I0684432

Salvaged Souls

Black Hills Wolves Book

By
Deena Remiel

This book is a work of fiction. Names, characters, places, and incidents are the products of the author's imagination or used fictitiously. Any resemblance to actual events, locales or persons, living or dead, is entirely coincidental.

Salvaged Souls
Copyright 2016 by Deena Remiel
ISBN: 978-1-68361-212-4
Cover art by Fiona Jayde

Published by Decadent Publishing Company, LLC
Look for us online at:
www.decadentpublishing.com

Black Hills Wolves Stories

Pleasure Me
Craving His Love
Jasmine Moon
Mating Dance
Amber's Ace
Wedding Moon
Bringing Down Romeo
Secrets of the Hunt
Salvaged Souls
A Wolf's Bargain
His To Protect
A Wolf's Choice

Winter Solstice Run

Wolf's Holiday
Winter Magic
Winter Secrets
Winter Solstice Ménage
Wolf in Winter Clothing

Murder in Los Lobos

Scent of Murder
Scent of the Hunt
Scent of His Woman
Scent of Madness

Also by Deena Remiel

Elixxir
Ghost of a Chance
Disquieted Souls

Salvaged Souls

When a new woman comes to Los Lobos, looking for a fresh start and a helping hand, she turns dominant black wolf, Parker's world upside down. Struck by her beauty and vulnerability, he's immediately consumed by her voice. One with which he's all too familiar. The seductive, tremulous voice of his red wolf, his dream lover who he'd give anything to rescue from a torturous life. His mind is slammed by the impossible implications, and he can't let her out of his sight until he finds out who she really is.

Shiloh has endured endless days and nights as a captured, forced mate of an alpha, chained to a cast iron stove, a vessel for all manner of unspeakable abuses. The only thing keeping her alive? Her black wolf, her mate, who comes every night in her dreams, soothing away the anguish, offering exquisite love and hope that one day an opportunity will come for her to break away. With her mate away on a trip, she just might have that chance.

Shiloh and Parker are two bruised souls, salvaged

from the wreckage of their tragic pasts, who find that love might finally set them free.

Dedication

To all the salvaged souls, SURVIVORS, of abuse

Dear Readers,

Welcome, readers! I've always been drawn to stories where people, whose spirits and souls have been broken, find a way to heal through their love of one another. It's so satisfying to watch characters learn to trust again, to believe again, and to let go for the first time so that a forever love may enter their lives. I believe Salvaged Souls is just such a story. I hope you enjoy all the highs and lows of this emotional story as much as I enjoyed writing it.

Deena Remiel

www.deenaremiel.com

Chapter One

How long had the beast been gone? With a tremulous finger, Shiloh traced along the crude etchings on the pine floor as she counted. Ten grooves. Ten blessed days of silence, of peace, of tranquility. Ten glorious days with no one kicking her in the gut, punching her face, or tromping on her as if she were a throw rug because they couldn't be bothered to step around her.

Enough days had come and gone for fresh wounds to heal while older ones scarred over. Enough time had passed for her skin to become sensitized once again, and she quivered with the agonizing anticipation of being reintroduced to her mate's brutal treatment when he finally came back.

Shiloh leaned against the wood-burning stove she'd been chained to, watching with morbid fascination as a squadron of flies buzzed like tiny vultures around her empty plate. Considering she'd licked it clean over a dozen times, the buggers would have to look elsewhere for a meal of their own. Her iron collar chafed the tender skin underneath as she lowered her weakened body to the floor.

She dreaded Josiah's return with every fiber of her being.

Couldn't he just die from drinking tainted water on the journey to finding his oldest brother, long thought dead? If not, then, maybe on his return he could be killed by some rabid porcupine. She held the same sentiment for his three brothers. Never, in her wildest imaginings, had she thought when she'd run away from her own pack, she'd wind up kidnapped, turned into a battered sex slave, and suffer indescribable indignities as a forced mate to the worst monster who ever lived on earth.

All she'd wanted, all she'd thought of, when she ran off that fateful evening was the freedom she'd gain from her clueless, cantankerous parents. They'd never been pleased with her, thanks to her wily siblings always setting her up to take the blame for their missteps. To stay with her family, her pack, meant a life doomed to repetitive failure and the misguided scrutiny of others. All of which would be well orchestrated by her sisters just to advance their own position and stake in their parents' favor and the pack.

Running away and being on her own had been a great achievement up until a couple of years ago, when she'd inadvertently passed into poorly marked territory of an unknown pack. Seeking a place to bed down for the night, she'd stumbled upon four large, mangy wolves. They'd never given her a chance to apologize, to run back to where she'd come from, or to find shelter elsewhere. Instead, they'd surrounded her, shifting into a motley crew of men. They'd punched her snout and ribs as they threatened death unless she shifted into her female form. She'd seriously considered death as a better alternative, but cowardice forced her wolf to submit, letting her human take over.

The teeth belonging to the one called Josiah had glistened with drool as he verbally claimed her for his own in front of the other men. With bound feet and hands, she was brought to the saddest excuse for a village she'd ever seen. The few houses still standing had seen better days. An acrid stench of rotting waste assaulted her nasal passages.

From that day on, no one questioned Shiloh as Josiah's property. The pack was so small, so ill-managed, they didn't even have a name. They came and went as they pleased. There was no organization or anyone who gave a damn. Josiah, the group-appointed alpha, had one main rule: *there are no rules except don't piss me off.*

When he'd introduced her to the pack, he'd let everyone know, in no uncertain terms, she was hands-off. First, he soldered the collar around her neck then pulled up the hem of her shirt for all to bear witness he'd marked her just above her right hip. As a last bit of degradation, he'd paraded her around like a dog. After her initiation into the pack, she became virtually invisible. Nobody in the godforsaken group gave a rat's ass about her or spoke a single word to her on the few occasions she was allowed outside. Only Josiah. He had many words for her. None of them nice.

She spent her days and nights in her female form, wearing a collar chained to the leg of a wood-burning stove with only enough run to make it to the main rooms on the first floor. She couldn't even reach the front door to answer it if someone knocked—not that anyone would. They'd just barge right in if they needed Josiah. They'd see her chained up but turn a blind eye. The chain-link collar squeezed her neck. So tight, if she shifted, she'd choke to death. She struggled daily to keep her raging wolf from taking over.

How much longer until the brutes returned? Her stomach growled its personal offense at not having an adequate food supply in the cupboards. Had he meant to come back sooner? Did something happen to spoil

4

his plans? What if he never returned? She touched the collar, her mind returning to repeated daydreams about breaking free and where she'd run to so she could settle down.

"Go on. I dare you to try again," she whispered. Her heart lurched as she wrapped bony fingers around the chafing shackle about her neck. A small tug yielded nothing. A stronger pull pinched at the already-tender skin. Yanking harder still produced no results, so she gave up.

"Sucker. Try pushing the stove over a bit. Maybe the chain can be freed." It wouldn't budge. She dropped her hands to her lap, defeated, then curled up in a tight little ball.

"I'm gonna die right here on this floor, in this shithole of a house, and no one is going to know or care." Giving in to the hopelessness, she closed her eyes, prepared to say good-bye to the only good thing in her life—the mysterious black wolf who'd been showing up in her dreams ever since her capture.

***

Shards of glass shelving crunched like cornflakes under Parker's feet as he wandered through Bread &

5

Butter, his grocery store in Los Lobos. Had a tornado hit it? An earthquake? No. A group of stealthy thugs had decimated his store, cleaned him out of his stock, basically wrecking the place.

When bad things happened, the true mettle of a person shone through. Some folks handled the stress better than others. Survival of the fittest. He'd been pissed as hell when he'd learned of the break-in, when he'd seen the destruction, but he realized it served him little to stew about it. He had a town that relied on his goods. That needed to be his focus. Ryker's team had found and dispatched the assholes rather quickly, which gave Parker a small measure of satisfaction.

His father had taught him right. *Take care of the people around you, son, because you never know when you're going to need help yourself.* Wise words from a father well loved for many years. It'd been just the two of them, helping each other grow up and taking care of each other as dominant wolves were instinctively wont to do. Father. Son. Buddies for life. Partners in crime and all things fun. He'd missed him terribly since that cruel day when a rogue wolf, a Magnum sympathizer, viciously killed him right before his young eyes during a father-son hunting trip. But, hearing his voice, even if simply from his memory, comforted him to this day.

Parker ground more glass into the wooden floor as he trudged to his phone book, the tedious process of ordering food, goods, and sundries next on his list. Cleanup could wait. His pack's needs couldn't.

"Hey, Bry. How are you?" His dairy supplier had been a longtime friend of his father's, so when Parker decided to open up a grocery store in Los Lobos, Bryan was the first person he'd called.

"Hey, man, what's up?"

"I need to place a huge order with you. I'm cleaned out completely."

"You're kidding, right?"

"Nope. There is no rotating of inventory, my friend. I don't even have an egg or a tub of butter left. I wish I could say it was due to amazing sales, but the store was broken into and trashed. So, get ready."

"Shit, man. I'm sorry. Just hope I have enough supply for your demand." He laughed lightly on the other end of the phone.

"Me, too." Parker ran down his list of products: fifty dozen eggs, fifty gallons of whole milk, twenty gallons of low-fat milk, and fifty tubs of butter. "Oh, and give me five large blocks each of American, Cheddar, and Swiss cheese, too."

"You weren't kidding! All right. Let me see what I can do for you. It's Monday. I've nearly run dry myself from the weekend haul. Give me about half an hour to get back to you. If I can't complete this list on my own, I'll find others who can help fill in my holes."

"My goal is to pick up the goods tomorrow or Wednesday. I'm hoping that's all right."

"I'll do my best. I'll talk to you later."

"Thanks. I appreciate it."

He called the meat purveyor next then the organic farmer for produce, and his distributor for the sundries. With everyone pitching in, he might be fully stocked by week's end. His ancient delivery truck was going to get a good workout. He brought it over to the garage for an oil change and returned to the store to start the massive cleanup.

Raking his hands through his long braids, he took a deep breath, shrugged his shoulders, and grabbed a broom. "This place may be an empty shell right now, but not for long."

He turned the radio on for some motivating music then shoveled every last crumb into a garbage can. His heart lightened while he mopped and grooved to the familiar tunes. The refrigerators still worked fine, as did the freezers.

Parker turned the negative into a positive, letting renovation ideas flood his mind. He could rearrange a bit. Maybe create a better floor plan. He'd thought about doing so a dozen times since he opened, but never had the opportunity to really evaluate in order to make any changes.

As more pack members returned, they'd need more goods. His store was the only full-service market in town, and expanding wasn't too far in the distance. Hiring someone to help would take the increasing load off of him. He added one more thing to his list of chores—put a sign up in the window asking for help. For now, though, he was a one-man army.

Chapter Two

A commotion outside her front door roused Shiloh from her lethargy. She stretched her chain to its limit to see what was going on. People had gathered on the front stoop. Had someone called a meeting? Josiah, as leader, had never bothered.

Frissons of fear coursed through her veins while prickles ignited across her skin. Had he finally returned? An unfamiliar male voice barked over the buzzing group. She strained to see, to hear what he had to say.

"Good evening, everyone. My name is Greyson. This is my mate, Willow. You've probably already figured out why I'm here. Your alpha is dead. I'm not going to lie. I'm the reason for the unfortunate circumstance."

Grumbles reverberated through the pack.

Josiah's dead? Had she heard right? *He's not coming back?* Dizzy from the implications, she swooned.

"I can't stand before you and say I'm particularly happy to be here. I'm here solely because Josiah and his family—my biological family—hunted me down. They tried to kill me. I protected myself. In the course of doing so, I had to kill them. When I learned of this pack, I was curious to see what I'd lost when my mother left me for dead in the wilderness. I thought I could come home to be of important service to you. So I stand here now as the new alpha of this pack. The alpha who should have been here all along. I stand here ready to help you, to lift you up and make this pack a thriving community for all."

Silence.

Inside Shiloh's jail of a house, she'd heard everything. Those words were like angels heralding her freedom.

"I guess you'll need a bit of time to let it all sink in. I can respect that. Just imagine, though, all you see here renovated. Imagine opening small shops to make this town self-sustaining. The sky's the limit."

Murmurs, grumbles, and laughter mixed into a powerful toxin against the proposed change.

"Check this out. He kills our alpha and thinks he's entitled to mess with what's not broke."

"Sounds like way too much work."

"Civilized living is for the civilized. Anybody here civilized?"

Hoots and howls of agreement from the crowd validated the various comments.

The stranger responded over the din. "Change is hard. It's easy to keep on keeping on in the face of adversity. But, sometimes, change is good. Like now. I'm placing the opportunity of a lifetime in front of you. All you have to do is agree to it. Accept me as your new alpha. We can change for the better together."

"We don't need a new alpha," a gruff voice from the group shouted. "We got a substitute right here. Ain't I right, Silas? Ain't you our alpha?"

Ugh. She cringed. Silas was just as bad as Josiah. Two peas in a pod. If Silas killed this guy in a battle for alpha, she could kiss her life good-bye. Silas would either leave her there to rot or force her to be his mate. The new guy sounded reasonable enough. Maybe a bit crazy for wanting to fix the hellhole of a village, but his heart was in the right place. What if she could find a way to get his attention and talk to him herself? Appeal to him as his brother's mate, a new member of his family. She could get instant protection if he stayed. If he decided not to stay, then maybe he'd agree to take her with him. She could be dropped off somewhere as far away as possible.

"Josiah named me alpha while he was away, so,

yes, I am the new alpha. There ain't no way in hell I'm givin' up my appointed role of this pack. So, I guess there's your answer, Greyson, The Wolf Who Would Be Alpha. Nice speech and all, but we're doing just fine as we are. Ain't we?"

The crowd agreed with cheers and hoots.

"We're here until tomorrow. Sleep on it, okay? Don't be so quick to run me out. I have a lot to offer. Give me the chance to show you why I *should* be alpha."

Footfalls on the steps told her the meeting was over. The group dissolved to points unknown. She'd lost her chance to save herself. Or had she? She waited and listened for the telltale revving of an engine to signal the pair's departure. None came. Instead, silence enveloped her. Desperate, she scuttled to the stove to reassert her energy and will to break free.

Simply trying to push the damned thing over hadn't worked. She needed a different plan of attack. Frustrated, she pounded her fists against the floor, sending a cloud of red dust into the air. *That's it! Why didn't I think of it before?* If she weakened the foundation underneath the feet of the cast iron stove, maybe the chain could slide out. All it sat on was a single layer of red brick. She could use a butter knife to chip away at the brick directly under one of the feet. There was a knife in the drying rack by the sink.

Renewed hope mixed with cautious optimism, spurring her on as she excavated for her life. "Come on, come on!" Bits and pieces of brick showered the living room, spraying her hair with a fine powder. Every so often, she nudged the stove to see if her work was paying off. The chain slipped free of its mooring. "Oh my God. Oh my God. Oh my God."

The long length of chain weighed her down. Given her frail condition, she feared she'd wind up buried beneath it before she could reach the outsiders. But, determined to exploit her only chance at freedom, she tapped into her last vestiges of energy and hoisted the coiled mass over her shoulder. Struggling to stand, she then shuffled to the front door as a free woman. Already hunched over from the weight of the metal, she dropped to the floor when the door creaked as she opened it. The clatter of the links hitting the floor clutched her heart with fear. Someone would be coming to see what had happened! She chided herself as she scanned the area. *Really? Exactly who would bother to check on me? No one.* She could scream the house was on fire. No one would give a damn if she burned.

Five minutes passed without so much as a howl, so she hobbled as quickly as she could to her ticket to freedom—an RV parked at the entrance to the village. She supposed it belonged to the strangers. None of the pack owned so much as a bicycle, but she'd heard the rumbling engine of some large vehicle earlier in the day. With a flattened palm, Shiloh rapped on the RV's door.

A man with a shock of pure-white hair and a furrowed brow peered out from behind the curtained window. Not a good sign. The door opened. The seeming disapproval on the mammoth man's brow softened into one of surprise. He took a quick scan of the area then stared at her, a question in his eyes.

"Please, let me in?"

He agreed with a wave of his hand.

"Thank you," she whispered, relieved. She scrambled past him, because, as much as she loathed entering the confined space, desperation won over fear. She sighed when her battered feet hit the soothing coolness of the vinyl flooring. "Please, hurry. Close the door." How ridiculous she must've seemed to him. It wasn't every day an unkempt woman, jingling and rattling, scrambled into a person's home. She sought a place amongst the furniture to hide, where no curious eyes could see her from outside. Crouching in the corner of the kitchenette would do. "No one can know I'm here, or they'll kill me."

"You're safe with us." The woman—Willow, she presumed—stooped down and flung her long, brown ponytail behind her shoulder, looking aghast at what throttled Shiloh's throat. "What's your name, sweetie?" Willow smoothed hair away from Shiloh's sweaty brow. The woman's gentle brown eyes sought to soothe Shiloh's frayed nerves. "What brought you here?"

"M...my name is Shiloh. I am...was Josiah's." She used the back of her hand to swipe at the tears beginning to well and pursed her lips. "He kidnapped me, bit me, forced me to mate with him. He's been keeping me chained to a stove in his house for...for two years, maybe? But today...today, I finally did it. I heard you talking to those assholes out there. When you said Josiah was dead, I knew you were my only chance to escape. Otherwise, I'd have rotted in his house." Her trembling caused the chains on her arms to rattle, underscoring the seriousness of the situation. "Please say you'll help me."

"Jesus Christ," Greyson muttered in disgust as he joined them on the floor. "Of course. Of course.

Willow, did this RV come with a pair of bolt cutters by any chance?"

"No, but you ought to know me by now. I go camping prepared for any situation. Give me a minute. I'll find them." She smiled down at him, nodding—a private message clearly exchanged—then scurried to a storage bin by the bathroom.

Greyson turned his attention to Shiloh. "How did you free yourself?" His tone held anger, revulsion.

"I've been working on pushing the iron stove over for days now, ever since he left to find you, I guess. Wouldn't budge. When I heard you speak today, it gave me an extra bit of motivation. I was able to dig out some of the foundation and move it just enough to pull the chain out from around one of the legs." She took a moment to breathe in deeply and calm her racing heart. "Thank you. Thank you for killing those evil people and coming here. I thought I'd never be free again. But I'm not out of the woods yet. Silas could claim me since Josiah's dead. I can't stay here. I *will* die. The pack isn't going to let you take over leadership. I think you know that already."

"I do. I won't fight for it, either. Had at least some of the members shown the smallest desire to get out from under this subsistent way of living, to make

18

something better of themselves, I would have considered it worth the risk. But I have a mate, the love of my life, who I must protect at all costs. Quite frankly, I can't live without her. If I were to fail in a battle to overthrow Silas, she wouldn't live beyond my last breath either. She's human."

Shiloh's jaw dropped. So focused on herself, she hadn't acknowledged the unfamiliar scent of human in the camper or even considered this couple's own trials and tribulations bringing them to her on such a fateful day.

"Wow. I completely understand. Maybe one day you'll share your story with me. As for these lowlifes, you're spot-on. There's nothing to be redeemed here. Except me. You're leaving tomorrow. Take me with you. Please? You can drop me anywhere far enough away from here. Then you can forget all about me."

"Sure, we can take you, but we wouldn't dream of dropping you just anywhere. You could run into the same unfortunate circumstance all over again. We can take you to your pack lands. Just tell us how to get there."

"No!" A fresh wave of tremors racked her body, setting off a cacophony of metal clinking against metal. "I left because I suffered other abuses there. There's no going back. Only moving forward."

"Okay, okay. Well, we can take you to our pack lands. You can become one of us."

"Is it like here?" Fear anew muffled the volume of her voice.

"No! People respect one another there. You would need to swear a blood oath of loyalty to our alpha, though."

"I-I can do that. I just can't...I *won't* live in a situation like the one I'm in now anymore."

"You have no reason to trust us beyond taking you out of here, but believe me when I say you will be safe and able to live a life free of harm."

Willow returned, bolt cutter in hand. "Here you go, Greyson." She handed it off and turned to Shiloh. "No more chains or shackles for you, missy."

"Thank God. My wolf won't hold up much longer. The bastard collared me as a woman, knowing if I shifted, it'd be too tight, and I'd choke myself to death."

A growl vibrated the air around them. Greyson's stormy demeanor helped make quick work with the cutter. As metal clipped metal, Shiloh gritted her teeth and closed her eyes while her heart thrummed in anticipation. Her shackles fell to the floor by her feet with a loud rushing *thunk*. Shiloh winced as she touched her abraded neck. A sigh escaped her lips as she looked down at the metal pile by her feet.

Free. She was finally free!

She shifted into her wolf and twirled around in place a couple of times, not quite sure what to do with herself. Turning to her saviors, she put her front paws on Greyson's chest to lick him. Willow patted her gently on her haunches. They both gave her wide berth to be. She howled but quickly stifled it. Chuffing instead, she bowed her head to the would-be alpha and his mate.

"Glad I could be of service. No one should be chained. Ever." He sat at the driver's console, hunched over the map. "You should stay with us tonight. You made it here safely, but who's to say if anyone will see you return to your house."

Shiloh shifted to human form. "Thank you. I don't think I could return."

"Can I get you something to eat or drink?" Willow drew the floral kitchen window curtains closed then guided her to the dining table. "How about a shower? Some fresh clothes? I think I have something to fit you."

Her stomach growled. "Sounds wonderful. I could

eat a grizzly right now, bones, fur, and all."

"I've got hamburgers and chips. Let me get you some water, too. While I fix you something, you can clean up. Follow me to the shower. Oh, wait. Greyson?"

He peered up from the maps.

"Can you grab me the emergency first aid kit, please?" She turned back to Shiloh. "Honey, you've got some serious scrapes on your neck. Once you've showered, I'll put some soothing ointment on them and cover them up so they don't get infected."

"Thank you. I can't believe it's really off. I could cry. I think I will. In the shower."

"It seems you've more than earned it. Come on." Willow grinned, urging her toward the rear of the RV. "Let's take care of you."

Chapter Three

"When she's out, will you tell her?"

Shiloh opened the bathroom door and walked out with steam billowing around her. "Tell 'her' what, Greyson?" She'd wrapped Willow's robe around her, making sure hardly any skin showed at all. Her long hair, once caked with filth, now draped over her shoulders in long, lustrous, fiery-red cascades. She'd curtained most of it over her left eye and cheek.

"We decided we're leaving tonight," Willow said. "Now, actually. No sense in staying any longer when his mind is made up."

"Thank God. I was dreading the hours until morning."

"Shiloh, can you tell us a bit about the pack's habits? Is it fair to say we can get out of here without anyone really noticing right now?"

Habits? They were disgusting, pathetic. Yes, she could tell Greyson all about them. "Most of the males are probably drunk off their asses. That's all they ever do come sunset. That, fight, puke, and pass out. All's quiet out there now, so my guess is they're done for the night. The few females here are either sleeping or hunting off to the west. I came from that direction. Lots of prey out there. Which way are we headed?"

"Southeast."

"Good."

"All right, then. Let's get going. The sooner we're gone, the happier I'll be," he said.

"I agree, honey. Shiloh, I fixed you a plate of food. Why don't you go to our room, relax, eat a little. You can even sleep for a while. We're going to be up most of the night, but you need to recuperate from your ordeal. This would be a good place to start."

"Okay, sounds really good. Thank you both. I can't believe this is really happening. If it wouldn't hurt so much, I'd say pinch me."

Willow approached her with warmth in her eyes, extending her arms. "You're safe. You're welcome. You don't ever have to be afraid of being hurt again." She hugged her gently then passed her the plate full of food and a tall glass of water.

"Just letting you know, once I'm done eating, I'll be shifting again. My wolf needs out, but don't worry. She's been cooped up so long, I think she's forgotten what it is to run. I'll just be asleep on your bed, as you said to do."

"All right. Whatever you need to do, you do." She offered her one last pat on the shoulder for reassurance then headed up front, by Greyson.

As they prepared to leave, Shiloh's heart pounded. Blood shushed in her ears. She refused to look behind the window curtains for fear of seeing any sign of life snooping around. Once they reached the open highway, she could relax in her seat and release her death grip on the armrests to eat.

"I'm ready to roll, sweetheart. Glad I parked this monstrous vehicle the way I did. I had a feeling we'd be needing to make a hasty exit at some point. We never should've come here. I had a decent life with the Tao. I don't need to be alpha to feel happy or complete. I have you and my job as tracker. That's always been enough. It always will be."

Willow took her seat next to him then buckled up. "Aw, I'm so glad you feel that way. But so sorry it didn't work out the way you'd planned. Their loss completely because you are totally alpha-worthy. But I trust what you sensed at the meeting. We knew it was a long shot. Don't regret coming, honey, because look what we gained. A sister."

"I think we made out much better in this deal." He turned the engine on and shifted into drive. "We saved a soul rather than a pack, but the soul we saved is worth thousands more than the weight of the rest of them in gold. Can you text Drew and Ryker? Let them know we're coming back with my sister."

"Sure."

One thing about RVs was the lack of privacy. Anything anyone said could be heard by all. While Shiloh devoured her plate of food at the table, she'd listened in on the couple's conversation, curious about the two people who risked much to help her escape. She wiped her mouth and took a final sip of water. As she headed to the rear of the RV, she shifted into her wolf then mounted the bed, grinning as she drifted off to sleep.

Scampering from the base of one pine tree to another, she stopped at each to groom herself, anticipating the appearance of her beloved mate. The black wolf, once he spied her, would no doubt fall victim to her beauty and intoxicating scent. She skittered about, anxious to see him, to tell him what she'd done this very evening. He'd be so proud.

Her nose twitched. A familiar honey-almond scent wafted through her nostrils. It could be only him. Closing her eyes briefly with relief, she smiled straight from her heart.

"My love."

"I am here." He stalked into view from the surrounding mist, an imposing figure, with piercing moss-colored eyes. He loomed large above as he leaned down to touch his muzzle to hers. "I've missed you."

"Me, too." She nuzzled and nibbled at his neck. "I have exciting news."

"Really? What is it?"

"I broke free tonight! I've been saved by a couple. They're taking me to their pack. They promised it's a good one. I'm free!" She bounded about him, over him, letting her joy go unfettered.

"Ha ha! Wonderful! I prayed this would happen someday. We must celebrate."

"I agree. With lots of lovemaking, if you can catch me!"

She nudged his side with her snout then dashed off, barking and howling with delight. It didn't take long for him to capture her, given their difference in size. Breathless, he pinned her to the ground to growl in her ear. "I believe I've won this chasing game."

"Oh, but, honey, in this game, we both come out winners."

They tussled playfully on the soft earth until he decided playtime was over. Mounting from behind, he mated with her in a jubilant frenzy. Replete, she fell asleep nestled within the warmth and protection of her black wolf lover.

***

Shiloh's wolf ears perked up, hearing voices speak in hushed tones just outside the bedroom. She no longer felt the soothing roll of the wheels beneath her. They'd come to a stop.

"Greyson, honey, are you okay?"

"Last time I saw this place, well, let's just say the pack cleans messes up well, but the ghosts still linger."

"I love you. We'll have many days to replace the bad memories with the good."

"Your words are as potent as any cure."

On four paws, Shiloh padded to the closet where shorts and a T-shirt had been set out for her. She shifted into her human form then changed out of Willow's robe and took a cleansing breath, steeling herself for the unknown. Opening the bedroom door, she was thrilled to find it hadn't been locked with her inside. "Are we there yet?"

"Yup. We're home," Greyson said. "Welcome to my piece of the woods, ladies. We're just inside Tao pack lands. On the very edge. You know me, Willow. I like my privacy. This keeps me, us, from being under a constant microscope."

"I get it, sweetheart. I love the idea."

Confidence be damned, a strong wave of nerves washed over her, flooding her brain with all manner of irrational thought.

"What's wrong?" Greyson hoisted Willow off his lap and stood, dwarfing Shiloh, like the little kid sister she'd become in this family.

"What if they discovered I escaped? What if they followed us here? What if they've come and are lying in wait to kill all of us?"

She retreated into a corner, a huddled, quivering mass, trying her best to dissolve into the cabinetry.

Greyson stepped into her space and kneeled beside her. He'd softened his voice, maybe so he wouldn't appear so intimidating to her. But he didn't need to. He didn't scare her. The others did. "Hey, Shiloh. We're in my pack's territory now. If they step one foot onto Tao pack lands, they're done for. My packmates have been on the alert ever since I was jumped by my brothers. We have trackers, like me, whose job it is to follow and disable any threat. Please calm down. You're safe with us."

She wouldn't budge. He stood, shrugging.

"Here, let me try." Willow took his place, offering a warm smile to which she gave a tentative one in return. "Shiloh, I know you're scared. You've been through so much. More than you've shared with us, I'm sure. Any threat to you has been killed. It would take too much energy, planning, and smarts to even think about coming after you. From the bit we observed about these people, they don't seem to care about much, least of all, someone who's been hidden away. Come on. Let me show you around our home. We have a lot of unpacking to do, but it can wait a few minutes."

She held out an authoritative hand as though expecting Shiloh to take it, the expression on her face similar to a mother's.

Willow stepped back, giving her room to extricate herself. As she did so, Shiloh's wolf came out and loped to the door. She turned around, snuffling, letting Willow know she was ready.

"I understand." Willow opened the door.

Shiloh took one tentative step down the stairs. Then another. Until, finally, all four feet touched the earth. She let out the smallest howl, more like a whine, and froze in place.

"Uh, honey," Willow nudged Greyson. "I think your expertise is needed now. Show her around as only a wolf can do. I'll unpack a hearty breakfast for us...or for me. Yes, for me. You go do what wolves do. Let her know her newfound brother is here for her."

"I could sure use a good run. My legs are starting to cramp up. This, I can do. I'll have her back—"

"I'll see ya when I see ya. Go! Do your thing!"

With a shiver and growl, he shifted into a white wolf then trotted down the steps. He growled at Shiloh then nudged her until she moved a couple of steps. He nudged her again, running around her. She moved a few more steps. He pushed her more, so she ran. She was much smaller than he. Not as quick. With his longer gait, he was able to catch up. Taking the lead, he showed her around his land.

He ran them by a stream leading to a waterfall and bluff then through the forested area where small animals scurried for cover. The tour gave her a chance to consider her new brother-in-law and what he'd done to his own family.

If Greyson could kill Josiah all over again, she'd love to watch. She'd record it so she could see it happen over and over again. If not for his inhumane treatment of her, then for his total lack of leadership that sank his pack to the depths of utter disgrace.

Chapter Four

This is just too easy, Shiloh mused as she continued on her first romp in two years. Nobody stopped them from leaving during the night. Nobody lay in wait to ambush them once they arrived at Greyson's home. Easy meant Shiloh'd better watch out because, just when things seemed to be going fine—*Bam!* You got kidnapped and chained to a stove for two years.

The white wolf was having the time of his life, running around like a nut.

Oh, to feel that free, that comfortable. She'd had a fleeting taste of it when she'd left her pack. She sighed as she loped along. Her sudden burst of energy at the start of the tour had waned. The plate of food Willow had given her was a mere morsel compared to what she needed to feel sated. To feel healthy again.

Out of sorts, she grappled with the fact she was free to roam, to explore, to be her own self without fear. Having been human for so long, her wolf tried her best to remember what it meant to *be* a wolf. Oh, she rejoiced at being let loose, but how did one behave after being locked away for two years? The open space threatened to overwhelm her poor animal. Greyson's gentle prodding throughout their run had helped a bit to find her way to her wolfish self, but she constantly scanned the area, searching, sniffing for any clues Silas and his buddies were nearby.

One more sniff. Something struck her. What was it? Rabbit. Salivating, she opened herself up to allow instincts to take over. And take over, they did, as though it were only yesterday she'd caught her last meal. She spotted the rabbit in the dense thicket. Stalking upwind from the small creature, she lay in wait as it neared her, unaware of its impending death. *One, two, three. Pounce!* She grabbed hold of the rabbit's neck, the warm, coppery elixir of life trickling down her throat as her teeth sank into flesh. It only took a moment for the rabbit to die. Maybe a couple of minutes extra for her to eat it.

With the taste of fresh meat coating her mouth, Shiloh hunted for more. Greyson watched her from a distance, probably sizing her up, judging her capabilities, trying to figure out what the hell to do with her. She had been held captive, her body broken and mended crooked. Her mind may be irreparably warped, but she still had good instincts. Hers said he was a good man and a good wolf. She downed a total of three rabbits before she approached him with a plan so he wouldn't have to think so hard.

Shifting into her human self, she asked he do the same. She watched his wolf shimmer and dissolved into human. "I know you've been trying to figure things out for me on this little trip around the homestead, so let me make this easy for you. You and Willow seem to be on the newish side of a relationship. I'd be very much in the way if I stayed in your home longer than a day or so. Tomorrow, take me to your alpha. Let me get this blood oath business out of the way so I can start living a normal life for the first time ever."

"Are you a mind reader? That was my plan, but not because you're in the way. Shiloh, my brother took you, forced you to be his mate. I can see the bond didn't take, but I will always consider you my family, my responsibility. I never had a family I could call mine, truly. You have given me the gift of a sister. You are, and will always be, welcome in our home for however long you need."

Tears welled, blurring her vision. She had to turn away. *I won't let anyone see me weak ever again.* She stomped her foot, swiped the hot tears from her face, and turned around to respond to this kind man's gesture. She pasted on a toothy grin. "You sure know all the right words to say, Greyson. They really cut to the heart in the nicest way."

"I've been learning a lot from Willow. She brings out the best in me, I guess."

"Lucky lady. Lucky man."

"I'll take you to town tomorrow. We have business to attend to now that we're back. I'll officially present you to Drew and Ryker. You can share your story, pledge your loyalty then we'll find you a place to live and work. With our growing community, there is no shortage of work to be done. I have a friend, come to think of it, Parker Bennett, who rents space above his grocery store. He lives in one apartment, rents the other...one bedroom, I think. We'll find out for sure tomorrow. It would be a perfect place for you to live. Store below you, Parker down the hall. You'd have your own space, but not feel so isolated as to be frightened."

"You seem to have everything worked out for me already. How is this possible?"

"If I had grown up with a sister, I'd want her to be safe, secure, yet free to experience the independence denied for so long. Well, I have a sister now. She's you."

"It's gonna take some getting used to. I have siblings. They are evil, manipulative bitches."

"I'm not evil or manipulative. And I'm not a bitch."

She laughed for the first time in over two years. "No, you most certainly are not. I see it's going to be a bit of fun having you show me the ins and outs of a real brother-sister relationship."

"Oh, the fun's not nearly begun. Wait until I introduce you to the matrons of the pack. They're a hoot! In all seriousness, though, we have a couple of pack members who can help you heal from the traumatic situation you found yourself in. There's no way to heal properly on your own. Many have endured similar experiences. One's even a certified counselor, so I hope you won't fight me on speaking with her."

She bit her bottom lip while kicking at the pine needles lying loose on the ground. Opening herself up? Talking about what she'd been through? Telling the basics was one thing. Going deeper, answering questions like, "How did that make you feel?" was not in her wheelhouse of tolerance. Dredging up the past to heal? The sooner she forgot about the last two years, the better. The past had been killed by Greyson, so no...fucking...way. But arguing with him about it wouldn't help matters.

"Okay, I'll meet them. It might be nice to meet people who aren't out to get me or blame me for their own failings. It could turn out to be downright refreshing to know not all women are possessed by the devil."

"Ouch. Those sisters of yours sure did a number on ya, didn't they?"

She just stared at him.

"All right, not going to discuss. Got it. It's getting late. Let's head to the house. I'm sure Willow's got everything set up by now. If not, we can help her."

"The thought of heading back is making my wolf antsy. I gotta run."

"So run. I'll be near."

"Thanks. Thanks so much for everything."

Had Greyson yet noticed the nasty scar trailing down her cheek? He hadn't asked her about it. Her wolf didn't care at all. She just wanted to run. Greyson shifted as well, giving her room without making her feel as though she were all alone. She wasn't quite ready to roam freely without an escort. That would come in time, she figured.

When they arrived at his doorstep, they morphed

into human form. She hesitated before entering the cabin, not sure she could cross the threshold. Fear of enclosed spaces, of doors closing behind her, had grown exponentially since her escape. The scent of chocolate and brown sugar set her nose to twitching, quelling her irrational thoughts, enticing her to enter. The aroma of baked cookies won the battle.

"Hi, you two! You're just in time. I'm about to take chocolate chip cookies out of the oven."

"That thing works?"

"Well, I suppose so. I preheated it. It beeped. It was hot when I put the cookie trays in. It must be working." She turned to Shiloh. "I have to admit, this is my first time here at Greyson's home. It's a long story, but we can save it for another day." Stepping into his arms, she peered up at him. "So, let me guess, sweetheart. You ate out a lot before you met me."

Shiloh watched him try to stifle a guilty grin. "Yes, but not in the manner you think. I eat at The Den a lot. I love Gee's hamburgers and fried pickles. Plus, I get to visit with him when he's around. Tomorrow, we'll take you there, Shiloh. It's a meal not to be missed. Besides, meeting Gee is kinda a big deal. Almost like meeting Drew, our alpha."

"I'm looking forward to it. If you don't mind, I

need to take a shower. I'm sweaty and grimy. A feeling I don't enjoy in the least. I think I'm going to be taking a lot of showers from now on."

"Just make sure you don't get washed down the drain," Greyson joked. "The bathroom's upstairs. You can't miss it. I'm sorry it's rather basic. You know, stall shower, sink, toilet. No style, but it works. Willow will have to wield her magic to transform it from a bachelor pad bathroom to something more pleasing to the eye."

"Oh, don't you worry about that, honey. I already have ideas. Shiloh, here's a fresh set of clothes for you. You can leave your grimy ones outside the bathroom door, and I'll see about cleaning them."

"Thank you so much. Greyson, don't worry. I won't look around too closely. I'm certainly not one to judge." Would a shower ever make her feel clean again? She wasn't sure. The one in the RV had served its purpose well enough, as this one would. The grime, the muck, the disgust, though, ran much deeper than the surface of her skin. Even if she scrubbed till she bled, it still wouldn't erase Josiah's touch, bite marks, cigarette burns, claw marks. Scars, seen or unseen, would last forever, therapy or not.

For tonight, she pushed all that deep down,

preferring to "unthink" while washing herself off from a day's hunting spree. She didn't bother to examine her body in the mirror. It was something she couldn't handle yet. *Sleeping arrangements will be interesting*, she mused as she dressed. There was only one room upstairs. It was devoid of any decoration but had a wardrobe and king-sized bed. Obviously for the two lovebirds. So she guessed she'd be sleeping on the couch. It didn't matter where she slept, really. She decided she'd shift to get through the night. It would serve two purposes—she'd feel safer as her wolf, and she'd be much more alert to any strange sounds exposing a potential intruder.

As she walked down the stairs, all clean and refreshed, giggling and kissing sounds emanated from the kitchen. She stopped halfway to the bottom, her heart aching at how lovingly the two spoke to each other. How desperately she wanted the same for herself, but she was way too damaged for it to ever become a reality. No one would be the least bit interested in a broken woman.

Josiah had shredded all of her hopes and dreams the day he began his brutal sexual assaults. He treated her as a receptacle for his primal rutting then beat the shit out of her afterward. She was used goods. No one in their right mind should want to get anywhere near her. She sighed, intentionally making lots of noise on the remaining steps, then tromped into the kitchen.

"Oh, Shiloh! How was your shower?" Willow beamed at her from Greyson's lap.

"Wet, thank you. I think I'll go sit by the window and let the air dry this thick mane of mine. It's grown so much in two years."

"Not a problem. We're just making dinner. Are you still hungry? We've made enough for three."

"I don't think I'll ever *not* be hungry again." She chuckled ruefully.

"We're going to need more groceries, so we'll make sure to stop in at Parker's Bread & Butter."

"Bread & Butter?"

"It's the grocery store," Willow offered. "Cute name, huh?"

"It does have a ring to it."

"Wait a minute. He has a couple of apartments upstairs, Greyson. But I bet you already thought of that, didn't you?"

"I told her we'd see about her living above it so she has a space of her own. Great minds, sweetness."

Sitting in the overstuffed chair, Shiloh's mind drifted away while her new family chattered and laughed in comfortable style. Rather than it going to a serene place, or finding a piece of beauty to stare at through the open window, her racing heart kept her mind tied up in an anxious knot, unable to appreciate anything. Even the cool breeze wafting through failed to calm her. Tomorrow would be the start of a new life for her. Wasn't this why she'd run away in the first place? Wasn't this what she'd hope to find at the end of her journey—freedom, respect, validation? So, why was she so frightened? Why did it feel suspect?

Given these past two nightmarish years, should I be surprised I'm questioning how smoothly things are going? But right here, right now, there was nothing to fear, nothing to worry about. Josiah had programmed her to fear everything and everyone.

Look out the window, Shi. Appreciate the beauty, the gift of a new life these people have given you, or, so help me, I'll beat the shit out of you myself. She raked her fingers through her hair to loosen the drying locks. She'd had enough of peering out windows to last her a lifetime. An antsy feeling suffused her body. Time to let her wolf out. She'd been difficult to contain ever since escaping. Shiloh understood and hoped, with time, the urges would lessen.

"Greyson, Willow, I'm going wolf. I'll be outside,

close to the house. I'll stay where I can always see it."

"All right. Have fun." Willow winked at her.

She shrugged and loped out the front door, around the front yard, listening, sniffing, acclimating to the area. Her wolf wasn't interested in running anymore. She just wanted to be, to at least pretend to be, secure. So she lay down on the porch to enjoy the cold breeze as the sun set. Her eyelids drooped, losing their battle to stay open. As she fell asleep, Greyson and Willow's groaning and growling lulled her to sleep like a lullaby.

Her heart beat furiously against her ribs as darkness enveloped her cowering body. Sniffing the air, she scented her mate close by. Longing and anticipation replaced the initial fear of isolation, yet her pulse raced stronger than before. Where was he? She needed him desperately.

"I am here, my cherished one. I am here," he howled in wolf song.

"Come to me, my love, my mate, my soul," she answered.

She could smell his approach; his latent power suffused the area with his scent, lighting the space around him as he sauntered closer. Glowing emerald eyes locked onto hers. She stood, emboldened by the nearness of her protector. She could face anything with him by her side.

The radiance surrounding him encompassed her as he touched his muzzle to hers. Exchanging love bites and licks, she welcomed him by nuzzling his throat, his jet-black fur so soft, so reassuring, so him. He dwarfed her tiny frame, and she loved the feeling of getting lost within his massive, thick-furred body.

"I thought I'd never see you again. I thought maybe you'd leave me once I was free. Maybe you'd think I wouldn't need you anymore to help me stay strong. But I do. I'll always need you."

"I'll never leave you. You are mine. I am yours. Do you know how many days I've awakened feeling so frustrated I could do nothing to save you? I'm so glad you're finally free. Keep beckoning to me in your dreams. I'll always come. We'll be with each other for eternity."

She howled a love song for him then, after tangling their bodies in mating, they huddled together in a loving embrace as they fell asleep.

"Shiloh, time to wake up."

She whined, snuffled, giving Willow her you're-wrecking-the-best-dream-ever look. It didn't work.

"Shiloh, we gotta get moving. It's a long way to Los Lobos."

She growled, stretched her legs then stood to shake away the cobwebs. Once shifted, she offered her newly dubbed sister a disappointed, sleepy glare. "I'm not much of a morning person."

"I can see." Willow chuckled then took a sip of whatever was in her mug. "Did you sleep well, though? Out here all night?"

"Yes, it was wonderful. The waking part, not so much."

"Well, if you like coffee, I have plenty in a pot ready to pour."

"I used to. I think I might cry on the first sip."

"It is a powerful bit of magic, that damned elixir. It's the dawn of a new day for you, my dear. All things possible, all things grand. I'm glad to be a part of helping make it happen for you. So, we'll leave within the hour. Greyson says he can get us there by noon. Should give us enough time to conference with Drew and Ryker first. Then we can meet up with Greyson's friend, Parker, to see about new living quarters."

Teeth and hair brushed, it was as good as Shiloh was gonna get. Her wolf took over, spending the entire

46

ride in the backseat of Greyson's truck, head out the window, mooning over her dream mate, who'd thankfully come to her during the night. She thought she'd lost him once she escaped. He'd kept her alive during her long captivity, visiting her nightly to cradle her in his protective embrace, mating with her, helping erase the emotional and physical damage Josiah had caused. At least, he did so in her dreams.

She guessed her brain was a mighty powerful tool for self-preservation. He'd said something this time that had her puzzled. If he was conjured from her mind while dreaming, how could he awaken from it? Bizarre.

"We're here, Shiloh," Willow said. "We're in Los Lobos. Once Greyson parks, we can get started on our to-do list."

Shiloh shifted then cleared her throat. "Great!"

Enough dreaming. Time to get her reality safe and secure.

Chapter Five

It's so different here from where I was just a couple of days ago. The contrast was striking. It looked like a *real* town, with houses, stores, a restaurant, even a school. Most importantly, the clean streets, freshly painted buildings, and people's happy faces proved people cared. They took pride in their town. A sense of calm washed over Shiloh. They hadn't lied. She would be okay. This place could work out.

She walked behind Greyson and Willow as they guided her through the town center. The first order of business was to meet the alpha to get his official approval. Would he be intimidating or welcoming?

"Here we are." Greyson trudged up to the front door then knocked.

It took a few moments, but a woman, a very pregnant woman, opened the door with a grin that quickly morphed into a frown. "Greyson, I didn't expect to see you so soon! Is everything all right?" She peered beyond him and waved at Willow. "Everything is how it's meant to be. In other words, it didn't work out in Washington. By the looks of it, all has worked out awesome for both of you. Congratulations!"

"Thank you! I'm so ready for our little pup to arrive! I'm sure you're here to see Drew, but he's over at Gee's."

"Would you mind if I used your bathroom, Betty? It was a bit of a long ride to get here. I don't think this human can hold out much longer."

"Oh, my goodness! Not at all. Come in, come in!"

The pair walked in, but Shiloh couldn't move. Meeting the alpha was one thing. Meeting his mate, in such small quarters, was another. Her body remained paralyzed, a statue.

"Oh, forgive me! This is Shiloh. Our newfound sister. There's a story to be told at another time. Shiloh, this is Betty, Drew's mate."

Willow beckoned her to join them inside. All Shiloh could do was shake her head. Her voice had left her. The very knowledge of how to form words, gone.

"Shiloh, you're welcome to come inside my home."

Greyson's brow furrowed. He lowered his voice to say something to the very pregnant woman. She nodded and walked out of view while Shiloh's guardians stepped over to her.

"It's okay. You can stay out here. We'll only be a few minutes. All right?"

She nodded, sucked in a deep breath, and rocked in place.

"I-I guess I'm a bit claustrophobic, huh?" She tried to make light of it then shifted into her wolf to hunker down where she stood. But there was nothing light about it. She could barely stand to take showers in Greyson's home, let alone sleep inside it. It seemed houses were a huge trigger for her right now. She'd need one for an address, but her wolf wouldn't tolerate living inside it. Given all she'd been through, whatever wolf wanted, wolf got. *That's one way around a problem. Heck, it's only been a day.*

Her nose found all sorts of scents to interest her. Nothing threatening, really. Werewolves just doing their business, but there was a definite undertone of urgency in the chemicals their bodies produced. As shifters passed her in human form, they turned to examine her, inspect her, size up whether she was a threat or inconsequential. She was used to being ignored, so this kind of close scrutiny unnerved her.

The constant drone of construction assaulted her ears. It came from all directions. *Lots of building happening here.* Growth? She remembered the concept, but hadn't seen it in action for a while. Growth was good. She could see herself blending in, disappearing into the fabric of the community. She could make connections if she wanted, or not. She didn't know what to expect in terms of relating to other people. When she'd escaped to Greyson's RV, she was desperate and had to trust them. They wound up working their way into her heart. How would it be to make friends when the only intent was to be sociable?

"We're all set! Let's go on to Gee's. Then we'll meet up with Drew."

She whined and stood to walk beside them.

"Oh, can you tell Drew to bring over a few hamburgers when he's done?" Betty called from the front door, patting her belly. "You don't want to know how ravenous I've been, even as big as I am!"

"Not a problem. Great to see you!" Greyson rested an arm around Willow's shoulder as they walked comfortably with Shiloh's wolf trotting behind.

When they approached a storefront, she hesitated. Greyson patted her on the haunches. "It's not a house, Shiloh. It's a bar. Come on. You might want to change first, though."

She shivered and shifted. "Yeah, I guess it wouldn't be sensible for a wolf to enter a bar. Anything I should know before I meet your alpha?"

"Just be yourself. If Ryker's with him, just know he's very serious. He doesn't take shit from anyone."

"Who's Ryker?"

"He's our enforcer. His job is what it sounds."

She took in a deep breath then let it out. "Here goes everything." For the first time that day, she led, but quickly learned she had no idea where she was going. "Um, maybe you should go ahead of me, Greyson."

"Yeah." He chuckled.

He marched them to the rear of the bar where he knocked on the office door. A muffled approval to enter signaled the beginning of her new life. Two men occupied the small room. One sat at the desk while the other leaned on its edge.

"Greyson, Willow, I'm surprised to see you here so soon. You've brought a guest with you."

"Drew, Ryker, we're as surprised as you but happy to be here. This is Shiloh, my dead brother's forced mate. Shiloh, this is our alpha, Drew. Our enforcer, Ryker. She has a story to tell and a plea. We hope you'll hear her out."

Drew sat up a bit more formally in his seat and sighed. "A story. We all have stories, don't we? Forced mate, you say? Stories with that kind of beginning are never pleasant. What kind of wolf are you, Shiloh?"

"R-red wolf, sir."

"Um, hmm. Belong to a pack?"

She bit her lip, accidentally drawing blood. "Well, you see, I—"

He held up his hand to stifle her.

"I'm sensing complications. I don't need any more complications, least of all a pack charging onto our lands hunting you down. Ryker, deal with this. I'm sensing a hungry mother-to-be. Am I right, Greyson?"

"Yup, you are. She wants a boatload of burgers."

"All right, well, by the time I return from bringing my mate her lunch, I want whatever Shiloh's story is to be explained and a solution ready for my approval."

"As you command it," Ryker said, standing.

Drew lumbered out of the office, leaving Shiloh shaken. She peered at the couple, only to find puzzlement on their faces.

Ryker leaned against the desk once again. He lowered his voice. "A lot's happened since you left, Greyson. We'll talk later. Right now, I need to know why you brought her here. What does she want from us?"

"Josiah, my brother and appointed alpha of my birth pack, kidnapped her then held her captive for two years. When we went to take control of the pack, they refused me. Just before we headed here, she came to us, seeking asylum, a fresh start. I suggested she join the pack by swearing a blood oath to Drew. I highly doubt the pack will come seeking her out. They have no desire to improve their circumstances or any interest in her whatsoever. I've taken over the role of guardian. I am formally asking she be allowed to live among us, as one of us."

"Please," she added, taking a step forward, clasping her hands together in a prayer. "I beg of you."

Ryker's face offered no clue as to which way he leaned. "Why didn't you return to your birth pack?"

"I'd already left my pack when I was abducted. It's not a healthy place for me to return to either."

"Hasn't your birth family been searching for you?"

"I left almost three years ago. In all that time, I never crossed paths with anyone telling me my family was searching for me. They are, I'm sure, as glad to see me gone as I am to *be* gone."

He grunted, scratching his chin. "You are willing to make a blood oath to our alpha?"

"Whatever I have to do, I'll do. I was told the pack is filled with nice wolves. Walking around, it feels safe here. I need safe. I need nice."

"When Drew returns, I will recommend you make a blood oath. Greyson, you are bound by the oath you made before you left. If you should choose not to live by the oath, I will be forced to kill you."

"Understood, but there is no need for a reminder. My heart, my loyalty, will forever be offered to Drew."

Drew returned without fanfare and took his place behind the desk. "So, what's been decided?"

"Shiloh is prepared to make a blood oath to you to join the pack. With your approval, of course."

"I see. I'm trusting any issues have been laid out and discussed. Give me your knife."

Ryker handed over his hunting knife.

"Shiloh, hold out your hand."

She did. Without ceremony, he slashed her palm and his own then clasped the two together. She winced but held steady. She'd endured much worse pain. Blood lost was replaced with a profound sense of coming home, of rightness, of calm.

"Swear your loyalty to me and to the Tao Pack."

"I swear my loyalty to you, Drew, alpha of the Tao Pack, and to the Tao Pack."

"It's done. Welcome, Shiloh." He directed his attention to Greyson. "What's your plan for her?"

"We're going to the Bread & Butter. We'll see if

Parker's in need of a worker and if he's got space to rent."

The alpha nodded. "He's a good man. I'm sure he'll help you out. As for you two, Greyson, anything I need to be concerned about, or have you closed the book on your birth pack to come home for good?"

"No concerns, and, yes, we're staying at my house. I'll start tracking again as soon as Shiloh's situation is resolved."

"Good," Ryker chimed in. "We need you out there."

Shiloh accepted a wad of tissues from Willow as Drew released her hand. "What's one more scar, right? This time, at least, I earned it for a good reason."

"Go ahead. Shift so it can heal," Greyson offered.

She didn't have to be told twice. As they said their good-byes, walking out, she hobbled for a few minutes on three good legs. By the time they arrived at the grocery store, she had healed. Shifting into her human form, she lagged behind as the others entered the store, breathing in deeply to steady her heart. If there was a job for her here, she'd have to get accustomed to being indoors without fear of getting locked in. A quick glance and confusion set in. If this was the store, where were all the goods?

"Hey! Greyson, my man! What are you doing back in town? I didn't expect to see you for a good couple of years or more."

Shiloh grabbed hold of the doorframe with a vise-like grip. A sound as rich, deep, and silky like the finest chocolate, filled her ears, causing a flutter low in her belly. The baritone timbre sought every nook and cranny in her heart, her soul. It wrapped them in a luxurious, protective cocoon. When she dared to gaze upon the man sauntering toward Greyson and Willow, she gasped, unable to navigate the incredible situation unfolding before her. *The voice. I'd know that voice anywhere. But who is this man?*

"It's...it's...." she whispered then pressed trembling fingers against her lips as words failed her. The world tilted as his eyes met hers. Puzzlement faded to concern on his beautiful face. Unable to endure the cataclysmic event any longer, she tapped out, sliding to the floor in a heap of semi-consciousness and then total darkness.

Chapter Six

"Shiloh! Wake up!"

A strong ammonia smell brought her around mighty fast. "Oh, that is horrid!" She looked around, confused. "What am I doing on the floor? What happened, Willow?"

"You're all right. You just fainted. Maybe the oath took a bit more blood from you than we thought. Parker's gone to get you some orange juice."

She wriggled upright to lean against the doorjamb, thoroughly embarrassed by her weakness. "Parker. Orange juice. In here? There's...there's nothing in here. You sure this is a grocery store?"

"I don't know what's happened, but, yes, it's the only one in town. I'm sure we'll find out once we get you stable."

The reason behind her fainting spell rushed over with a small bottle in his mammoth-sized hand. "Here, drink this. It'll help." He smiled as he offered it to her. Careful not to touch him, she responded in kind as she accepted the bottle.

"Th-thank you," she stammered, paying way more

attention to her drink than to the man who'd given it to her. She had to be having a waking dream. This was not possible, at all.

She pressed the lip of the bottle to her own and drank deeply. It tasted real. If she was truly dreaming, she wouldn't be able to taste, would she? If she was really awake, then she better get her shit together because there was no way in hell she'd share what raced through her mind the moment Parker Bennett spoke.

"Feeling better?"

She blanched. *He's talking to me again! Answer him, damn it!* "Uh, yes. I think so. I guess I won't be donating blood any time soon."

He laughed.

His chuckle sent a rush of tingles from the base of her neck down her spine. The fluttering down low kicked into high gear. She groaned then waved off the concerned glares. "I'm all right. I'm all right."

"Maybe we should do this tomorrow, Greyson. She doesn't seem okay to me." Willow coddled her, like a mom would—at least a mom who cared would. She wasn't used to that.

"Honestly, just give me a minute. I'll be perfectly fine. Like this never happened." She shooed everyone away from her and stood on her shaky feet, beaming at her success. "See?"

"So, Greyson, this isn't just a friendly visit, I take it?" Parker turned to his packmate.

"We would've stopped by anyhow, but there's a bit of business we'd like to conduct with you. First, let me make introductions. Parker Bennett, this is Shiloh, our sister-in-law. She just joined the pack a few minutes ago. Shiloh, this is Parker, owner of the Bread & Butter."

Shiloh waved meekly. "Hi. Thanks for the OJ. I feel so much better." *That's it, girl. Finally found your tongue and your sensibilities!*

"Pleasure to meet you. Welcome to the pack."

Greyson stepped forward. "I see you've got a sign in your window seeking help. I think we found it."

"I can't even begin to tell you how much hiring someone would make my day, Greyson. A couple of days ago, I put in a huge order to fully restock the place. I'll be picking everything up tomorrow. There's no way I can stock the shelves by myself quickly enough to suit the needs of the pack. I need to be up and running as soon as possible. With help, I can make it happen."

"She needs a job, long-term, but if you only need her for a little while, at least it would help both of you out while she finds something more permanent."

"I need permanent full-time help, actually, so you came at just the right moment, Shiloh." He turned his full attention toward her. "Do you have any experience working in a store?"

Holy shit, I don't know how much longer I can keep it together! I don't know who the hell she is, but I'd know her voice anywhere. I just don't know how it's possible.

"I don't, but I'm a fast learner and work hard."

"Then I think I can take the sign out of the window. You got yourself a job."

"Great!" She clapped her hands together, thrilled at how well things were going.

"There's something else we wanted to ask you." Willow rested a warm hand on his arm while flashing a smile to melt even a hardened wolf's heart.

He already scored a major boon with hiring this woman. What more could make his day, or totally ruin it? "Yeah, what's that?"

"She needs a place to live. Do you have an apartment upstairs she could rent?"

Oh, this is a definite make-my-world-heaven kind

of day! "I do. I do. I've got the furnished studio apartment available. I live in the one-bedroom down the hall."

"Can she afford the rent by working for you?"

"Rent? I won't accept anything. We're off-the-grid here, so the bills are covered by sales. When you're here for a while and on your feet again, we can talk about a token. If you like the place, you can stay as long as you need."

Greyson offered him a hearty handshake. "This is why I love the pack. Quality through and through."

"Thank you so much, Parker." *God, her voice!* Her sweet, tremulous, sultry voice reduced his innards to mush. "I don't know how many times I can say it. All of you. You're incredible individuals. From having less than nothing to having it all. I-I feel so blessed." The emotion she so clearly tried to contain revealed itself in the waver of her voice, slamming into his heart like a boulder. He coughed just to breathe again.

Willow hugged her and swiped at her teary eyes. "Let's go see the place then we'll go buy you some clothes. I guess you'll have to wait until tomorrow for Parker to pick up everything else you'll need to live."

"I have some basic items in my apartment upstairs to tide you over until you can shop in the store. Free of charge, of course."

She gazed down at her shoes. "You're too kind."

Dang, why is she so shy? "Nah, just like to take care of my own."

"Great, someone else who thinks he can possess me," she mumbled, rolling her eyes at Greyson and Willow. "If it's all the same, I'll just stay down here while you two check it out."

Oh, boy. A woman with issues. But, then again, what shifter doesn't? He let her first remark pass without comment as he led his friends upstairs. After Greyson, Willow, and Shiloh checked out the apartment and formalized the agreement with a handshake, they walked out of his place to the clothing store.

He collapsed against the doorjamb. *What just happened here?* He pinched himself. "Ow!"

Yeah, he was awake. The woman with the voice of his dreams just barreled into his life, and he was helpless to do anything but *everything* she wanted or needed.

How crazy is this? Unbelievable, really. He wouldn't be telling a soul about it either. He had no idea who the woman was, but her voice, even with the little bit she spoke, had brought his dream lover to life.

He'd had to stop himself from closing his eyes as he listened to her. There was no doubt in his mind or heart. This woman's voice possessed something supernatural. How else could he explain the likeness? The woman clearly needed him.

He liked being needed. He needed to be needed. As a dominant in the pack, it was in his DNA to protect and take care of his own. She was very much *his*, even if she didn't know it or want it yet.

So, what had brought her here? Slight of frame, even a bit on the skinny side, as though she didn't eat much. Was it by choice or by circumstance? He would enjoy showing her the ropes and getting to know all about the woman with his dream lover's voice.

For now, though, he'd have to work on controlling the unabashed lust her voice elicited from him. It wasn't her fault. She had no idea what she'd done to him just by speaking. Adrenaline coursed through his veins like a raging river. He could run a hundred miles in five minutes flat. He was sure of it. He might have to consider using earplugs around her. Roaring with laughter, he checked to see if anyone was nearby to hear him.

Back in the store, he closed the door. Things were going to work out. The store would be fully stocked again. He'd be open for business with Shiloh to help out.

Shiloh. Her name meant peace, tranquility. Had she brought it with her, or was she here to find it?

***

I just might find some peace for the first time in my life. He'd given Shiloh the task of making shelf tags for the big haul, and she found pleasure in the menial job. Feeling useful, needed was an important step in her healing process. She may not want to talk about the past with a counselor, but she understood the importance of moving on. Of taking steps to embrace her independence again.

With help, she had a place to call home and a job to keep her self-sustaining. She'd been on the cusp of doing the same years ago. Having taken music classes all through school, she'd acquired singing gigs around town. She thought she'd enjoy a life of making people happy with her original songs. When her sisters pulled the rug out from under her, they decimated her career. She decided to leave her family and visions of fame behind.

Now, she could be who she wanted to be, do what

she wanted to do, and make a difference in her own small way for this community. Yet, the very idea scared the living shit out of her. A knotted-up ball of jumbled emotions left her a hot mess. *One step at a time, little girl. One step at a time.*

What were those steps?

Get through this next minute. Write your tag, set it aside. Pick up another one. Get through the next minute. If that's what it takes, do it.

So the afternoon waxed on to evening without her seeing neither hide nor hair of Parker after he explained what she needed to do. Oh, she scented him all right. He was everywhere and nowhere, but never in plain sight. Greyson and Willow had left for their neck of the woods a few hours ago. But not before a lot of debating if they should stay in town for the night to make sure she was okay. After assuring them she'd be fine, she'd said her farewells.

A sharp, stabbing pain in her belly reminded her food was essential for a malnourished body. But where to go? Gee's seemed to be the place, so she packed up the supplies and arched her back in a well-earned stretch. Hopefully, they'd be willing to start a tab for her so she could eat now and pay later. She hadn't realized how long she'd been sitting there, hunched over the table, but it had been long enough for an ache to develop between her shoulder blades.

"Hey," a deep, rumbly voice broke through the silence. "I'm heading out to Gee's for din—"

She quickly drew her arms in, bumping against the butcher block table. She'd known he was there in the background. His distinctive scent had grown stronger just a moment before, but she jumped just the same.

"I'm sorry. I didn't mean to scare you."

"Oh, that's okay." She nonchalantly tipped her head a bit forward to cast a curtain of hair over her scarred cheek. "My fault. I guess I'm a little skittish in this new place."

He glanced around, his mouth as wide as an open garage door. "Wow! Look at how much you got done! Did...did you finish?"

Heat crept up her neck to her cheeks, which she deftly concealed with her hands. "Yeah. It's not hard to write labels or hang them up. Anyone can do it."

"Anyone didn't get the job. You did. You're amazing."

"No, I'm not."

"Okay, you're not. You're fantastic. Now, as I was saying, I'm headed to Gee's for dinner. He's the only

68

place for burgers and fried pickles, so if you're hungry, we can walk over together."

Panicked by the offer, her defense mechanism responded for her. "No, it's okay. I'll go a little later."

"Listen, I'm not asking you out on a date or anything. I'm simply saying we can go there together, order our meals separately, and sit separately if you want. Or, we can break bread together. Suit yourself. Not trying to box you in or make you feel uncomfortable. Quite the opposite, actually."

She bit the already-swollen part of her bottom lip, considering his offer. Was she over-analyzing? Freaking out for nothing? Probably. "Okay."

"Okay?"

"I said *okay*."

"Okay, let's go." He clapped his hands together. "Day is long gone. Everything's ready for tomorrow's haul. Time for lights out and a relaxing evening."

As she passed through the doorway, his hand glanced over her shoulder. Instant quakes erupted at the point where it touched. She flinched. Had he noticed? Felt it? If he did, he didn't show it. Closing the door, he locked it behind them.

Gee's was down the main thoroughfare. About a three minute walk. Three interminable minutes of walking beside *the voice*. Since it was dark out, all she could really do was listen to him, as he seemed to disappear into the darkness. She'd gotten to scrutinize him earlier, immediately noting his skin color a dark chocolate with the slightest tinge of blue. Did he have tattoos peeking out from the collar and his shirt sleeves?

Besides Greyson's snow-white skin, she'd never come across anyone with as unique a look as Parker before. She figured it had something to do with his wolf genes. His skin glistened with dew, accentuating the thick, sinewy curves of his muscular arms. With his long braids gathered in a band, beads of sweat highlighted strong cheekbones and a squared jaw. Beads caressed his upper lip, defining its bow shape. And his eyes, oh, his eyes! They shone like the brightest emeralds. Just like....

She shook her head. He was a beautiful specimen of man any girl would die to have as a mate. She sighed as her new reality, her new beginning, splashed ice water over her heated veins. *He's gotta be a dominant, with the way he instantly took care of me.* Although he'd left her alone to work, she'd felt his presence so close she didn't know whether to be grateful or feel suffocated. She didn't sense him to be another Josiah, but personal space seemed a precious commodity to her now. *He's definitely unmated. He'll have no use for broken, damaged goods such as I am anyway.*

She'd admired from afar, taking comfort in his dreamy voice during the day. During the night, however, she prayed her dream wolf lover hadn't lied and would still be waiting for her despite her newfound freedom.

"You all right over there? You got awfully quiet."

"Yes, I'm fine." Not really. Her legs ached. Going from no exercise for two years to running left her out of shape and breath. "I guess I'm not used to all this walking."

"All this walking? Gee's is like three minutes away," he laughed.

She stopped mid-stride. "Let me rephrase. I'm not used to all this *human* walking." She blanched at her misstep but trudged on, kicking herself in the ass for not thinking before she spoke.

"So, you're gonna throw something like that out there and leave me hanging?" He caught up to her then passed her to walk backward as she continued.

"Forget I said anything."

She shivered, shifted then ran the rest of the way

until she reached the bar, disregarding the ache tearing through her muscles. She changed to her human form and ordered two hamburgers with an order of fried pickles. By the time Parker sauntered into the bar, her order was ready. Points for him for giving her space because the walk shouldn't have taken more than a couple minutes. He sidled up beside her, flashing a knowing grin. She offered him a guilty smirk as she shouted out, "He's buying. Thank you!"

With the to-go bag firmly in her mouth, she morphed once more and ran out into the street, down to her new home. She hurried up the stairs, through her tiny apartment to the balcony then sat down to eat the best hamburgers and fried pickles she'd ever tasted.

Leaving Parker stuck with the bill hadn't been very nice of her, she knew, but he would've offered to buy her meal anyway since she had no money of her own yet.

He unsettled her. Shook her up something fierce.

He'd expected her to open up to him, but she was nowhere near ready to do anything of the sort. Free enough to share her nightmare existence? Not likely, ever. The past needed to die in the past and let her live in the present. *Next time you open your mouth to say something, don't!*

Chapter Seven

Parker was certain he'd entered another dimension. When Shiloh had shifted and run away, he could have sworn she'd turned into the very red wolf he'd dreamed of for so long. To possess his dream lover's voice *and* to look like her? Well, those two things were far too coincidental. How could one *dream* a mate into being? Was it even possible? He'd been so stunned she'd left him to pay her bill, which he would have done anyway, he'd let her get away from him.

The situation deserved answers. He was primed to get them. He pounded down the few hamburgers he'd ordered then shifted to run to his place to confront her. He slowed his pace as his storefront came into view then trotted the rest of the way. He turned the corner to get a good view of her balcony. There she sat, his red wolf dream lover. *It can't be her! It doesn't make sense!*

She spotted him, stood abruptly then leapt from her balcony, down to the ground where she took off, running.

***

She had seen the bewilderment in his eyes. He had questions. He'd wanted to talk. Feeling cornered all over again, the only thought in her mind had been to escape. So, she'd taken a risk and leapt from her balcony to charge off into the wilderness. What was happening here? His voice could bring her to near orgasm, his body, too luscious not to ogle. Yet, her mind refused to acknowledge her carnal reactions, so she ran from him.

He'd been drawn to her, too, but why? What could she possibly have to offer him—or anyone—for that matter? Working and living so close to him could only spell a disastrous mistake. One she'd rectify in the morning. She'd find another job. Let her wolf live in the woods. She hated being inside anyway. They'd see each other around town, when she'd need to buy groceries, but their awkward magnetism would eventually fade. It had to.

Out of breath, she slowed down by a stream and followed it to a waterfall where she drank, rested then had a good whine and howl session. She should have known things were going too smoothly. As her tears ebbed, a song she'd written years ago, documenting her unfortunate circumstances, came to mind. She'd sung it numerous times in her head while chained up in Josiah's house. Did she dare sing it aloud? She figured herself far enough out of town that if she sang softly no one would hear. So she started her mournful lament to a life she longed to live but always out of reach. To any critter passing by, it probably sounded like a sorrowful wolf song even though she'd written it as a human. When she finished, she dipped her snout into the stream. As she pulled her head up, a strong scent wafted past her nose into her brain, her heart, and her soul.

He's here. My dream lover is here. But where? How is this possible? It must be her senses playing tricks on her. Longing for him, she dove, head and heart, into the delusion, skittering around in the underbrush, tracking his scent. It seemed to be emanating from everywhere. Was he stalking her, corralling her like prey?

She blinked a few times as she peered into the darkness of a thicket to find a pair of glowing emerald eyes staring intently at her. Startled, she yowled and leapt a few feet off the ground then turned to run.

Unfortunately, she ran out of land.

Skidding and scrambling, she used her claws to

grab at whatever would keep her from plummeting off the cliff. Thankfully, only about five feet down, her long nails dug deep into the tree roots jutting out of the cliff wall. Howling, she had no idea what to do next.

"Shiloh!" Parker yelled down to her, leaning over the edge. "Stay put! Stay wolf! I'll get you!"

Parker? What? How? Nothing made sense except for her precarious position.

She whined and nodded. He reached down, but she was too far away for him to hoist her up. "Dammit! I'll be right back. Don't move!"

As if! A lifetime later, it seemed, he returned and tossed a looped vine over the edge. He managed to hook it around her neck. "Put it under your front legs, one at a time. I'll hoist you up!"

She did as he bade her. Before she knew it, he had her lying safely upon land once again.

"Holy shit! Are you all right?" He scrambled over to her as she shifted and rolled onto her back.

Spurning all of his attempts to examine her, she whipped the rope from around her. "Yeah, I-I'm okay." She sat up, confused. Pissed. "You're the reason I nearly died just now. Thank you very little. What were you doing? Following me?"

"What? I...." His jaw dropped, his eyes widened, as though affronted. "I'm the reason? So, it's my fault you're so skittish? Excuse me, but I got no owner's manual with directions on how to deal with your sensitive nature when you walked into my store this morning and turned my world upside down."

She stood, fired up even more. Oh, this man pushed all the wrong buttons! "Owner's manual? I *am* not and will *never* be owned by *you* or *anyone ever again*! Now, wait just a minute. I turned *your* world upside down? I thought I saved the day. You said I was amazing. So you're a liar, as well as too damn nosey."

"Nosey?" His baritone voice rumbled low beneath the cacophony of forest sounds. So deep, so controlled. He inched closer. She retreated, waiting for a fist or an open palm to kiss her cheek. "How about interested? How about concerned, Shiloh? How about caring and giving a damn? Do those words fit anywhere in your vocabulary, because it's what drove me to follow you tonight."

"Aha! You admit it! You *were* following me." Triumphant, Shiloh pointed, branding him with her pointed finger, regaining her full stature.

His quiet ranting stopped. His voice took on the tenor of boyish yearning, dislodging her from the solid ground she thought she'd stood firmly upon. "Then I heard your wolf song and, well, it hit me like a dagger to my heart. Not to mention your voice. I was helpless to do anything but listen to your seductive, soulful, aching voice."

Her human had become unable to navigate around his confusing words any longer. She growled low, letting her wolf take charge. Incredulity washed over his face. He dropped to the ground.

"So *there* you are. It explains everything, actually. I can't believe it, but there you are right in front of me. You really *are* my dream wolf lover, aren't you?"

She chuffed, staggering in retreat. *What did he say?* He shifted into a wolf with thick, black-as-midnight fur and muscled haunches. His appearance, she knew all too well. Every curve, every angle, every piece of him. He connected to her mind then continued. "Do you recognize me now? You must. I can't be alone in this extraordinary happening. I can't be going crazy. Tell me you know who I am now, Shiloh."

She whimpered, not believing what her eyes, ears, and nose begged her to. Could he really be the black wolf from her dreams? The one who kept her alive each day she'd been held captive? "Parker? I...I...."

"Tell me, please." He whined, desperation dripping from his words.

Holy hell. What do I say? What do I do? What if, when I respond, he disappears like a ghost in the mist? I have to say something. I owe him at least that much.

"Yes! Yes, I know who you are. But how is this possible? I must be dreaming. It's the only way this makes sense. I'm having an elaborate, lucid dream. This isn't really happening."

"Oh, but it is very real. Believe me."

She shook her head, as if to shake the impossible from her mind to see clearer. "You're the only thing I *do* believe in. The only one who's kept me sane and alive all this time. But, if this is only some sadistic game someone's playing on me, us, I'll die. I tell you, I *will* die."

Prancing around her, he howled. "Sadistic game? How about a gift from the heavens? How about you let go of the fear now? Begin your new life, with me." He stopped in front of her, resting his muzzle on top of her head. "It is what we always wished for...to be real for each other so we could live and love together."

She closed her eyes as she breathed in his familiar, soothing scent. "I know, but—"

79

"But what?"

"Things are different now."

"In what way?"

"Parker, you know what I've been through. I-I'm damaged goods. I'm so damaged a thrift store wouldn't put me out on the floor for sale."

"I know what you've been through. Every brutal second of it. It tore me apart each morning I awakened, knowing I couldn't do anything to help you. That's why this makes sense now. I can be everything you need me to be, everything you want me to be. I can protect you, fight your demons for you, and kiss love back into you. Only, it won't be a dream anymore. It's what you want, isn't it?"

She shifted into a woman and stood before the black wolf, taking a deep breath, knowing this would be her last attempt at shaking him up to see reason. She trembled as courage and resolve spurred her to a new level of boldness. Lifting her shirt off, she then unclasped her bra to toss it aside. She unzipped her pants then wriggled out of those and her panties to stand naked before him. She painstakingly turned around, arms outstretched.

"Look carefully, Parker, at what you *say* you want. Take a good long perusal at the scars across my back, my ass, my legs, my breasts, my face, these arms. Scars you couldn't see beneath my fur. *This* is what you want to sign up for? *This* is what you want to see each day? Each night? God! I can't even glance at myself in a mirror, and yet you stand here wanting *this*? I won't say yes just to satisfy your dominant urges to protect, when the mere sight of me can make anyone gag with revulsion." Tears streamed down her cheeks, unbidden, hot. Disregarding them was the only way to stay strong in the face of imminent rejection.

Parker shimmered and appeared, tall, broad, with muscles vibrating their latent power. She cowered, crouching low to the ground. Seeing him as a man broke the mystique between them. It left her painfully vulnerable.

"You would show yourself to my wolf, but not to me? We are one and the same." He stepped toward her to gently grab her battered hands in his broad ones. "Stand up, Shiloh, so I can see your woman again."

He pulled, his command speaking to both her wolf's soul and woman's heart. She unfolded to stand upright before him.

"Your beauty only begins at the surface. It goes down deep to your core. Every night you returned to me, I fell more in love with your fortitude and determination to find a way out. To live again. Your silky red fur may have hidden these scars from me, but I knew when each fresh wound arrived. They're battle scars, badges of honor to celebrate living through hell and coming out victorious. You're my mate in our dreams. Be my mate, Shiloh, for real. I promise to bless each one of those scars every day because they're what brought us together."

She stood numb, speechless, as he released her to remove his shirt.

"Wh-what are you doing?" Trembling turned to quaking.

"I'm showing you who I am as a man. Your man."

"I-I can't. Don't. I'm afraid." She scrambled to her pile of clothes and gathered them to hide behind.

"Oh, baby, don't be frightened by me. I'm still your wolf. Your protector." His eyes flashed a brilliant jeweled glow, giving her a long glimpse of familiarity. "Let me chase your fears away." He kept his jeans on and sat on a patch of grass as he extended a hand, beckoning her to join him. "Come sit by me, love. It's okay. You know me as your wolf. Come get to know me as your man."

Conflicted, she stood paralyzed by remembered brutality at the hands of another. Yet her soul cried out to run to him, the man whose wolf she'd fallen in love with. The one who she credited her survival throughout Josiah's reign of terror. She couldn't turn away from him, but she couldn't go toward him either. "I can't move. I-I can't move my legs. Parker."

She reached out a hand, and he jumped up to seize it, as if to capture the most fragile butterfly. "I'm here, baby. I'll always be here." He kissed her fingertips then brought them to flatten against his racing heart. "Can you feel my heart pounding? I'm nervous, too. I want to do right by you. I want you to feel safe. I want you to feel secure with me and want me as wolf or man."

She choked out a sob, stepped into his space, and touched her forehead to his chest. "Oh, God, I need you so. Help me find my way to you. Help me not be afraid." She shifted into her wolf, whining a heart-wrenching sob as she released her womanly frustrations to relax into her wolfish ease.

He changed, as well, sidling up next to her to lick her snout, imposing his strength upon her. "Let's just lie here together for a while, my love. It's okay."

She nodded, at a loss for words for her most cherished love then nuzzled his neck while doing her best to lose herself within his massive coat. Closing her eyes at last, she lapsed into a calmer state as Parker rested his limbs securely around her.

At first, she didn't know what time it was when her eyes fluttered open, but the moon told her it was nearing midnight. Awareness was slow to return, but as she flexed and stretched, she realized she'd changed into her womanly form at some point while she'd slept. She peered down to see Parker's human arm draped across her hip, his leg across hers. He'd fallen asleep beside her. *Extraordinary!* How profound her wolf let her woman loose to feel and be with him.

She turned ever so gently in his embrace. Not to wake him, but simply to gaze upon him. The softness around his eyes. The chiseled features of his strong jawline. The archer's bow of his lips set slightly apart. How could she ever fear this man? This man, who was completely devoted to her. It wasn't the man she feared at all.

Josiah had a chokehold on her mind and body. Tactile memory kept his brutal hands like a thin coating across her skin, acting as a shield against Parker's kinder touch. Somehow, she needed to rid herself of the monster. Carefully extricating herself from Parker's cocoon, she crept to the stream, grabbed a fistful of brush, and dunked it in the cool water. She needed something rough, coarse to scrub herself down.

She rubbed the makeshift loofah over her entire body. The first pass didn't seem to do much good, so she did a second round, a bit harder this time. It had to work! Tears fell hot on her cheeks as she went for a third pass, even harsher than before.

"Hey, sweetheart. What are you doing?"

She continued scraping her skin free of the revulsion that had welled within her.

"Aw, babe, stop. You're hurting yourself."

So wrapped up in the throes of loathing and despair, she hadn't noticed Parker's approach. Gasping, she curled in on herself, turning away so he couldn't see her self-inflicted damage. "As long as I remember his touch on my body, I won't feel you. I'm trying to get him off me. It's not working, damn it all. It's not working."

He crouched before her and stayed her hands. Easing her fingers open, he removed the twigs and pine needles, replacing them with kisses on her bruised palm.

"Trust me, Shiloh. I'll remove all memory of his hands on you. It was something I couldn't do before, when we met in dreams. But I can do it now. I'll do so for as long as it takes. I swear to you." He bent his head, peering under her curtained hair to connect with her waterlogged eyes. "Will you let me in, sweetheart?"

She placed her abused palm on his cheek, nodding, praying he could deliver on his oath. He cradled her in his arms, lifted her off the ground then carried her to their soft, earthy bed to set her down.

He removed his jeans to stand before her, large, powerful. A study of the perfect male human body. And he was as naked as she.

"See me. Know all I am and have is for you. There's not a part of me that can or will ever hurt you." Her wolf shimmered across her skin, ready to take over. His voice, stripped as bare as his body, pierced through layers of scar tissue around her heart. "Please, don't run from me."

Never had she felt more at war with herself. Did she dare trust this man? Why shouldn't she? He'd been with her for two years now, albeit in her dreams, but still. She needed him like the air she breathed.

"The only place I'm running is *to* you." Dried needles crunched under foot as she bravely stood and invaded his personal space. His arms enclosed her like a security blanket.

"Thank God," he sighed into her hair.

Her eyes shuttered closed as their human bodies touched for the first time. Such an exquisite touch, a soothing touch, a healing touch. So new a sensation. A new experience for them both, considering they'd only ever met in dreams, and only made love as wolves. She breathed him in, his familiar honey-almond scent. It had cloaked her, comforted her each night as they came together. She stood, frozen in his embrace, afraid to move for fear of other less-kind images invading the sanctified moment.

He stroked her hair and leaned back to push aside the strands she used to hide from the world. He laid his lips to her temple, her eye with a slash through its outer corner, and then feathered light kisses along the remaining scar line down her cheek.

Her heart thundered through her body as her breath quickened. Her red wolf strained to come out. She missed his wolfish touch. Jealousy threatened to derail the intimate moment.

As if he could sense it, Parker growled low by her ear. "Shhh, you are not forgotten, my love."

She would not settle or be appeased by the notion her lover would join with her soon. She wanted him now. "Parker, we've only known each other as wolves.

Mine won't let me have you until she has yours."

"Then we'll let our wolves have their way because mine is begging for yours, too."

She shifted in his arms, knocking him over. Before he hit the ground, he'd changed, as well. They tussled, nipped, and lapped at each other as though their separation had been a lifetime. She trotted to the stream and beckoned him to play. Finally, they made love as wolves, finding joyous release together. When they regained their strength, they ran through the stream again, but as they came out, their wolves gave way to their humans. Still hot with need, their bodies slick with mountain water, Parker took her into his arms and kissed her feverishly on the lips. She'd never experienced anything as explosive, as liberating before.

Wanting so much more from her lover, she put her arms around his waist and trailed her fingers up his muscled back. His tongue teased her mouth open. She capitulated, while silently thanking her wolf. She'd paved the way for her human side to enjoy his human touch, a simple act defiled and corrupted by Josiah's carnal, deviant ways.

Parker devoured her neck with his hot mouth and seeking tongue. "Mmm, let's go to my place where we can continue this on a soft bed."

Alarms rang through her love-soaked brain. *A bed. A bed is inside a house.* "Let's stay out here. I don't care much for indoor activities. We have a perfectly good bed right here." She pointed to the patch of grass by the stream.

"I know what you're doing. You can have your way for now, but mark my words, I'll teach you how to enjoy being inside my home, in my bed."

She'd think about that another time. Right now, all she wanted was to be wrapped in his arms, feeling protected and loved. Yet, fear had begun to worm its way into her heart.

He swooped her off her feet to walk them over to the soft, grassy patch. He laid her on it and caressed her cheek as he gazed deeply into her eyes.

Chapter Seven

"I promise to permanently remove the fear still haunting those pretty amber eyes of yours." He kissed each of her eyelids as they fluttered opened and closed. "I promise to erase his vile imprint from your mind, your heart, and your soul. I will sanctify your body with my love and protection. Every day, until the end of time, I will do all this because I love you with every breath I take. Every fiber of my being."

He kissed her tears as he eased himself down to rest beside her. Gathering her to him, his hands took a painstaking journey across her chilled skin, seeking, it seemed, to learn every inch of her body and normalize the touch of a man who truly cherished her. Each touch of his hand sent her on a dizzying ride of intense fear, dissolving into waves of sensual desire. Searing heat coursed through her veins, causing her to squirm in his arms, wanting to feel so much more, yet terrified of what might happen.

Trusting him to hold true to his promises, with gentle prodding from her wolf, she gave in to the pleasure and rapture of their human lovemaking.

Tipping her head back, she kissed his chin. Wriggling higher against his hardened body, she cupped his face to kiss him with unabashed ferocity. He was so ready for her. Had they been wolves, they would've already mated multiple times. But the human in him took his time with her, something she appreciated.

He definitely appreciated her body. His tongue blazed a trail across her collarbone, down around her breasts to her sensitive nipples, while his fingers set trails of their own, creating tiny explosions of electricity across her belly and inner thighs. He never hesitated when his lips or hands approached one of her scars. Instead, he spent more time on them, kissing each one. The slashes from Josiah's claws on her buttocks were still red and healing. The wounds he'd inflicted across her body would never disappear since she'd never been allowed to shift to her wolf. So, the memory of his touch would eventually be erased by Parker's tender ministrations, but not their visual markers. A cruel irony, to be sure.

"Stop thinking, Shiloh. Unless you're wondering what I'm about to do for you next. I'm not sure, but I'm guessing you're mighty tasty." He kissed her soundly, taking her breath away, and licked his way down to where she'd gone wet with need. "That's it.

Let go with me, sweetness."

"Oh, my God," she murmured, his hot breath on her mound causing her to weep down there even more. "I didn't know it could be so good." No man or wolf had ever made her feel this way before.

"Mmm," he growled, vibrating against her swollen lips then teasing her clit with the tip of his tongue.

Groaning, she bucked. He did it again, lingering a bit longer this time. He lapped, sucked, and repeatedly thrust his tongue inside her. She whimpered as she grabbed at his shoulders, raking fingers across the expanse of his back. Waves of ecstasy, like a tsunami, drowned her, and she cried out his name as she climaxed. *So this is what it is to truly make love.* She'd never experienced this until now, this very moment. He crept his way up to lay gently atop her.

He was huge, ready, but he didn't enter her. "Are you okay?"

She nodded.

"Are you ready to do more? I won't do anything you don't want."

"Yes, set me free, Parker. Set my woman free to love you." She spread her legs apart, opening for him, needing him inside her so desperately to erase the horror, to replace it with heaven. She grabbed his ass with both hands, guiding him toward her as they locked lips. He fought against entering her fully, though.

"What's the matter? What did I do?"

"Nothing, honey. I don't want to hurt you. You're tiny, and I'm...well, the opposite of tiny."

"Parker, I need you inside me. Please, don't worry. Let our bodies make the magic."

He eased the tip inside her. She groaned with relief, with anticipation. He pushed a little farther, and she reveled in the pleasure, the ecstasy. Deeper he went until he was fully sheathed by her.

"Holy shit, you feel so good, woman." He slid out then thrust in.

He set the pace deep, slow until he pulsed inside. Then his thrusts quickened, turning erratic. A sheen of sweat coated his smooth, sculpted body. Suddenly, he pulled all the way out.

"Turn over onto your stomach."

Fear washed over her, a whimper escaping her lips. The present disappeared as the past took hold of her mind. Josiah never asked. He always manhandled her, manipulated her into any position he wanted, regardless of her comfort, and shoved it in any hole he could find.

"No, no, not that. Not that," she sobbed. "Please no, Josiah."

Parker leaned in close so all she could see was his face. "Shiloh, return to me, baby. Come on. It's me, Parker. You're safe. I'm with you. I'll make it all better."

Parker's concerned face and soothing words broke through her flashback, returning her to the present. "I-I'm okay. I'm okay now." She nodded. "Replace the horror with love. Replace the horror, Parker." Turning over, she offered herself to him.

"We don't have to. Are you absolutely sure?"

"Yes. Make love to me, Parker. This way, every way."

Raising her up to rest on her knees, he held her hips in his strong hands, entering her slowly at first, but when she moaned her approval, he increased the pace. She cried out as waves of orgasmic bliss racked her body. He continued to thrust and groan his rapture until he climaxed, too.

"Mine!" he half cried, half howled.

A sudden stabbing pain on her left hip caused her to flinch. "Aah! What the fuck? Oh, my God! Oh, my God!" Her world spun as he pulled out, collapsing beside her. She folded herself nearly in half to see what he'd done to her. "Son of a bitch, Parker! Son of a bitch! What have you done? You marked me?"

Outraged, she scrambled to her feet. "Sleazy, good-for-nothing, slime balls who want to possess everything around them." She whipped around to face the object of her ire, still lying half-comatose, oblivious to the major infraction he'd perpetrated against her. "How could you do this to me? I told you I'd never be owned by anyone! You've ruined everything for us. Everything! I trusted you and your pretty, human words. My God, you destroyed everything we'd created. Don't bother trying to find me. You won't! If you do, you won't like what greets you."

She grabbed her clothes and ran off toward…toward…. She didn't know where. Just not anywhere near him. Deeper into the woods she ran until her human legs gave out on her, so she shifted to run even farther. Fury coursing through her like a jet engine, she howled as she'd never done before. Anyone listening would know to steer clear, give wide berth, and don't fuck with her.

She came upon an overhang perfect as a place to crash. The cave was shallow enough to see if it was occupied, yet deep enough to provide ample coverage from the elements. As it had started raining, it was the best bet to keep her dry. Her wolf inspected the area, sniffed around for any unwanted creatures then settled in for the night. Fat chance of her ever shifting to human again! Her red wolf would protect her from now on.

***

What the hell just happened? Parker sat up on his elbows, helpless to do anything but watch Shiloh run off. He'd already pissed her off. Not listening to her demands would make everything worse. Amidst a flurry of mumbles and exclamations, he tried to make sense of it all. From what he understood from her spewing, he'd royally screwed up.

But how? They'd promised themselves to each other every night in their dreams. He'd told her, unabashedly, how committed he was to her in every aspect of their lives. She'd agreed. They'd made love, for real, both as wolves and as humans. So what went wrong?

I bit her, marking her as my mate.

But it's what all couples do.

I said she was mine.

Shit.

He'd completely ignored her fervent demand to be her own woman, which she'd stated in an earlier conversation. She would never be owned by anyone ever again. *But marking isn't about owning one another. It's about proclaiming to others that* no one else can touch. Her perspective had been skewed, no doubt aided by Josiah's treatment of her. He should have listened to her better, though. He never should have assumed their coming together gave him permission to assert his claim on her. *I'm not a wolf or man. I'm a pig.*

Fuck, and double fuck.

If she didn't come around eventually, there would be problems. Big problems. For both of them. What he'd done couldn't be undone. Somehow, her thinking needed to be rewired on the matter.

He hurriedly dressed to track her scent then rethought his strategy. Going after her right now may not be the wisest thing to do. It could wind up backfiring. Instead, he would give her space, a chance to mull things over on her own.

With a heavy heart, he returned to his apartment above the grocery store and watched from his window as dawn arrived. As much as he wanted to go to her, he had to care for his pack. Today was pickup day. It promised to be doubly grueling considering he had no one to help him anymore. He sighed, got up to shower and dress then started his arduous journey to all of his providers.

As he drove down the main road through town, pack members emerged to cheer his return. The hero had come home victorious and laden with treasures. He knew how important this load was to them. Parking around the rear of the building, he turned off the truck and hopped down from the cab to begin the tedious process of unloading. He unlocked the roll-up door to reveal his treasures. Grabbing the first box, he turned to bring it inside.

"We thought you could use some help." Blocking his way stood Kole, Max, and Jasper, with arms opened wide and broad smiles on their faces.

"Are you kidding me? You guys are awesome. Thank you!"

"Just tell us what to do or where to put things. We'll have this sucker unloaded in no time."

"Well, these first few rows of boxes can go straight to the front of the store. Place them in front of the labeled shelves they go on. Man, I can't tell you how much I appreciate this."

Ryker and Saja came around the corner. "We're here to help, too! Our pack needs your Bread & Butter. You need us. It's mutually advantageous to get you up and running, I would say."

One by one, in pairs, in groups, the town showed up to get their Bread & Butter fully stocked. Caleb, Mitchell, and Rio showed up. Brick, Chance, and Julie; Paul, PG, and Kennedy; even his alpha, Drew, all came to lend a hand. Parker's heart swelled with pride and love for his Tao pack. He divided them into two groups, the outside team, unloading the truck, and the inside team, stocking the shelves, refrigerators, and freezers. Once the truck was empty, those outside joined the inside team. In a few hours, his grocery store was filled to the max, ready for customers. It was a miraculous event. One he'd never forget.

Even Gee stopped by with trays of cheeseburgers and bowls of fried pickles to feed the army of helpers. As packmates slowly cleared out, he found an opportunity to approach the bear. If anyone could help Parker fix the mess he'd created, he could.

"Hey, Gee, do you have a few minutes to spare? I need your sage advice."

"I have time. Come to my office when you're ready."

"Thank you, for everything."

Gee nodded and left.

So, when the last of his packmates shook hands to leave, he left, too, heading straight to The Den. Paul tended bar. "Hey, I'm here to see Gee. Is he in his office?"

He nodded and jerked his thumb over his shoulder.

"Thanks."

Parker knocked. A grunt came from behind the closed door. Assuming it meant for him to enter, he did. "Hey, thanks for seeing me."

"I can't help but see you. It's an eye thing. No need to thank me. Advice? *That* you can thank me for."

Laughing lightly, Parker sat down across from the old bear. "Gee, I screwed up royally. I don't know what I can do to fix it."

"Must be about a woman. When men screw up, it's always about a woman."

"Guilty as charged."

"So, what have you done?"

"You've met Shiloh, Greyson's sister-in-law, right?"

"Yes, such a wounded little pup."

"This is gonna sound crazy, but our wolves have

known each other for about two years now. In dreams."

Gee's brow rose.

"We became lovers, in our dreams. Crazy, I know. In those dreams, I became her reason to hope for a solution and an end to her captivity. When Greyson showed up with her, I couldn't believe she was real, that our relationship had come to life right before our eyes. But the proof wouldn't be denied. She acknowledged the same when we finally came together."

"Sounds like all should be well, then. You were lovers in dreams. You can be mates for life."

"Exactly what I thought. She agreed. But it's all gone to hell."

"What's happened?"

"We mated."

The werebear grunted.

"I marked her, Gee, as any mate would, but she saw my claiming as owning. She'd spoken vehemently against ever being owned by anyone, since Greyson's brother had held her against her will. I got that. What I didn't expect was her equating claiming with owning. She freaked out and ran from me. I know where she is, but I'm not sure if I should go to her. She made it pretty clear I shouldn't ever again. I love her. She's my mate. It's gonna get increasingly difficult being apart from each other. I don't know what to do to get her to forgive me."

Gee grunted again, rocking in his chair. "Skewed perspectives lead to much misunderstanding."

"Yes."

"This little pup needs special care. You should have known better."

Parker hung his head in shame. His wolf followed suit. "You're right. I should have known. Damn it."

"It is a rough road you travel. You must seek forgiveness for being a brute. You must enlist the help of a female to guide her in understanding the claiming. And you must honor her, not just with words, but with action. Good luck. You will need it."

After opening a file on his desk, Gee started punching on his calculator. Parker had been summarily dismissed. He stood, and as he left, shut the door behind him.

Paul knocked on the counter, drawing Parker's attention as he walked past. He wrote furiously on his notepad. *Damn, you look like you just got a verbal beat down! Need a drink to soften the blow?*

"Nah, rain check. I deserve to feel this sting a good

long while. I'll be by later, though, for dinner and that drink."

Paul wrote again. *I'll make sure it's a stiff one.*

"Later, dude."

Paul waved good-bye.

Parker walked to the store, hoping against hope she'd returned. She wasn't downstairs. When he trudged to her apartment door, he listened, but utter silence met him. *She has to come back, doesn't she? She would need to wash up and change her clothes, wouldn't she?*

He slumped against her door. *Not if she stays wolf.* It frightened him beyond measure. The longer she stayed wolf, the harder it would be for her to shift to her human form. Given the fact her wolf hadn't been allowed to surface for over two years, he wasn't so sure she'd be willing to relinquish her newly realized freedom.

Ask forgiveness. Get help.

He'd get the help she needed first. It would hopefully pave the way to redemption. He called on a friend of his parents, Zamirah, to ask her to go to her. A telepathic empath, she could probably connect with and understand Shiloh's inner dialogue. The sage woman agreed to meet him downstairs in his office.

"Thank you so much for coming, Zamirah. Have a seat." He offered her his office chair.

"Thank you, Parker. Not a problem." She eased herself down onto her seat with a minor groan. "So what's the plan?"

He leaned against the edge of his desk. "I'll take you as far as I tracked her. Then you'll have to go it alone. There's no way she wants me anywhere near her right now. She's shifted to her red wolf, last I knew, but we'll see. I need you to help her work through some heavy mind shit she acquired while being held captive for a couple years. The biggest one, the one that sent her running, is our mating process. What it means to be mated. She thinks it's all about ownership, and it's freaked her out. Houses also cause her stress. She won't go inside them if at all possible."

"Tall order, there, mister." She stood, grasping his shoulder to give him a bit of a shake. "I feel terrible for what she's gone through and what she's still going through. I'll see what I can accomplish. If she's willing to listen today, hopefully, she'll continue to do so tomorrow and in the days to come. So, tell me, where is she?"

"Nearly to the border of the pack lands. Zamirah, you gotta make this work."

She offered him a confident grin as she tapped his cheek gently. "I'll do my best, honey."

Chapter Eight

Shiloh hadn't wanted to draw attention to herself, but she needed to unload. So much had happened over the course of just a couple days, her head swam. Captivity, freedom, love, betrayal. It was all too much for her. Singing helped her calm down. If Parker dared to track her, she'd tear his heart out to eat it for dinner. Not really, but anger, hurt, and confusion left her unpredictable, so who knew what she was capable of doing in the heat of the moment?

With the rain having diminished to a few stray drops, she sat on the overhang to continue her melancholy song. The sound of shifting leaves and needles underfoot silenced her. Her ears perked up. Catching the scent of a stranger frightened her. "Who's there?" she snarled, scrambling about trying to locate the intruder. "I hear you. Come out! Show yourself!"

"Don't be afraid." A small, gray wolf with tinges of silver around her face stepped into view from the thick underbrush. "It's only me, Zamirah, a Tao pack member. I'm a friend of the Bennett family."

"The Bennett family?" She growled as she made

the connection, "What do you want? Did Parker send you here?"

"I won't lie." The wolf took another step closer. "He asked me to come. I agreed to, willingly. Shiloh, I know what you're going through. I've had my own struggles with trauma and PTSD. It took a bit of time to feel normal again. I imagine normal for you is an abstract idea at the moment."

Shiloh chuffed her agreement. "He's wasted his time. You can go on home."

"I'd rather not. He may have asked me to come, but I want to stay because I see so much of who I was in you. If you let me in a little, I can help you. Someone helped me, so I believe in paying it forward. What else have you got going on tonight besides that lovely singing? Give me a chance."

"How do you suppose you can help me?"

"I'm a telepathic empath. My abilities allow me to go beyond those walls you've created for self-preservation to get to the root of your issues. Once there, I can help you accept, release, and sculpt a new, healthier perspective on the world. Would you like to live a healthier, happier life, Shiloh?"

Pent-up emotion choked her. She coughed. Maybe getting help wouldn't be so bad after all.

No! Paranoia held her tight in its grasp. Not from anyone remotely tied to Parker. They had their own agenda.

She shook her head vehemently. "No! Leave me, now!"

Zamirah lowered her head, whining. "I'll do as you say, but each moment you don't face your demons, they grow larger, more dangerous."

"Go!" Shiloh barked, threatening to pounce on the smaller, ancient wolf.

Zamirah shrank away and ran off, leaving the broken red wolf alone with her raw, untamed emotions.

Shiloh howled with reckless abandon then broke into a wolf song she'd never sung before. It came from the depths of her wounded soul crying out to any who would listen.

"Shiloh," a new, softer voice whispered seemingly from the ground. "Shiloh."

She twirled around to find the body to the voice, but failed. "What now?"

"Shiloh, come."

The disembodied voice seemed to emanate from inside the cave she'd holed up in. She scooted off the overhang, cautiously peering inside. A warm, inviting glow drew her in. As she reached the center of her shelter, the air around her shimmered. At the rear of the cave appeared a golden wolf.

"Shiloh, my pup. I am Aquene, your spirit guide. Your desperation called to me, so here I am. Come sit by me."

She obeyed, like a reluctant child to its mother, but each step toward the glowing wolf filled her with more confidence and curiosity. "I was desperate in my captivity. Where were you then?"

"You had your mate. You had no need of me. But you need me now. It is clear."

Shiloh scrutinized the visage in front of her. "You...you remind me of my great-grandmother. Her voice. Her grayed fur. I loved her so much."

"It is so. I believe you are ready to transcend your current circumstance. To move forward, you must go back." She tapped an insistent paw on the ground beside her.

Mesmerized, helpless to do anything else, Shiloh did as she was bid.

"Relax. Let me in. Let me see and feel your inner world." The spirit guide set her muzzle against Shiloh's forehead. The red wolf watched in a stupor as Aquene pulled away, nodded, or frowned every so often. "Well, my dear one, you've got a lot going on up in that head of yours, don't you? Want to just forget your childhood? The past two years? Push it all down and out of sight, huh? Literally, out of mind?"

"Th-that was my plan, yeah."

"Won't happen," the sage wolf scoffed. "Not this way. You're headed down a self-destructive path. Houses not your thing anymore? Give it time. This overhang won't be either. You'll suffer brutal winters outdoors, risking death before finding an enclosed dwelling. Shiloh, shelter isn't your enemy. Josiah was. He used his house as a jail to hide you and his nasty dealings from the world. But he's dead now. You can choose to enter or leave any building you wish of your own accord. You can choose to make an enclosed space warm and inviting. You are in control, not Josiah."

Shiloh whimpered. "I've been so afraid the doors I walk through will lock for good behind me. I'm sure it sounds crazy to you."

"Not crazy. A natural response given what's happened to you. But do you see how skewed your perspective is? Do you see how you now have the freedom once denied you?"

She considered, ruminated, and let that thought

settle in her mind. She now had freedom once denied. "Yes, yes, I do."

"Every day, walk into buildings or friends' homes in town. Stay inside for as long as you can then choose when to leave. Even if you start out only able to be inside for a few minutes, increase the length of your stay the next time. You will reduce the fear by creating a new, positive reality to replace the old nightmare."

"I see your point. I think I can do it."

"Good. You can always count on your friends to help you with this, too. Now, there's one more hurdle you need to jump, Shiloh. It's a pretty serious matter. Let me ask you. How are feeling right now?"

"Honestly? I'm still angry as hell at Parker."

"Okay, anything else, my dear?"

"I would imagine you know already. You wanna hear me say it, don't you?"

Her spirit guide just stared at her.

"I'm about ready to jump out of my skin. Okay? I'm feeling all sorts of lusty inside. All I can think about is making love to him until I go blind. It's pissing me off. I hate him for what he's done to me."

"What he's *done* to you? You've *both* experienced a *miracle* here. You literally dreamed each other into your worlds. You've connected on another plane, professed your love for each other, and mated by mutual consent."

"He bit me, marked me, and made me his own. He knew how I felt about it." She bristled, thinking on the moment.

"A statement uttered under the breath or in a heated argument, left unexplained, isn't exactly being transparent, Shiloh. It's simply confusing."

That smarted as strongly as a smack to the face. She couldn't deny the truth of her statement. "I see your point."

"As with houses, you have an inaccurate perspective on our mating ritual. I'd like to explain it to you, so you can move on with or without Parker. I'm not here as his advocate. I'm here as yours."

"Go on."

"While making love, true mates will bite or mark each other. You believe it to be a sign of ownership, but Shiloh, Josiah's influence warps the truth of it. It's about proclaiming to the world this wolf is loved and protected by you. No one should threaten the bond or else suffer deadly consequences. You didn't bite him, and you don't have to. But by marking you, he's cast a shield of protection around you so you never have to fear again. He will always be your strongest supporter, providing for you in all ways. Does this sound like ownership or a loving relationship you'd like to have in your life?"

Shiloh sank to the ground and rubbed a paw against her forehead, stroking it down her snout. "I've made a big, ol' mess of everything, haven't I?"

"No, not in the least. You've only awakened from a nightmare to find a knight in shiny fur waiting for you. It's time to let Parker be the one for you."

Restless and anxious to make things right, she stood up to pace the cave. "I need to go."

"Yes, you do."

She stopped mid-stride. "I can't stay wolf forever, can I?"

"No, you need to share your time with your human. Remember, she didn't stifle you. Josiah did. You both have the power now. You both are in control. Haven't you been hidden away long enough? Compromise to make this relationship work."

Shiloh's human itched beneath the surface to be released. "If we run, we can make it to town before midnight."

"Good choice. Time for me to go. When you need, use your wolf song to call me. I shall come."

"Thank you, Aquene. I think you may have just

saved my life."

"I look forward to seeing you live it!" She howled and romped about Shiloh then faded into the cave wall, leaving Shiloh alone to race toward her future.

She hadn't noted where she was going when she bolted, but she thought Parker'd been close a time or two, so as she suspected, his residual scent led her straight to him. It was a long way back, too. By the time the moon reached its highest point in the sky, she came upon the Bread & Butter. Would he be there?

No lights shone in the store, but what about his home? She'd have to go around the side to open the door. She'd have to go up the stairs and down the hall to knock on his door.

The door to his apartment.

Where he'd hopefully invite her in.

And she'd walk inside without hesitation.

Taking a deep breath then exhaling, she shifted into her human form to take the stairs two at a time. *Please be home. Please be home.* The only thing separating her from the love of her life was his damned door. So many things could go wrong with just one knock. *But so many things could go right!*

Clenching her hand into a loose fist, she rapped on the door and waited. Not a sound from beyond let her know he'd heard her. She checked behind her, verifying a path for a quick exit then knocked a little stronger. "Parker, are you in there? It's me, Shiloh. Parker?"

Was that movement she heard? A faucet running, maybe? "Damn it! Parker, open up! Please!"

Openhanded, she slapped at the door, over and over, finding not the least bit of enjoyment in the irony of being locked out instead of locked in.

"Let me in." Sobbing, Shiloh leaned her forehead against the door, wishing she could be a ghost and pass right through it. Exhausted, utterly defeated, she turned around and headed toward her own place, as her wolf. A door opened, and her ears perked up.

"Shiloh?"

He *was* home! He'd heard her! She spun around as she shifted to her woman, elated and frightened all at once. Opening a door was one thing, forgiving her another. What a vision he was, though, standing in the doorway, towel wrapped low upon his hips, his dark-chocolate skin dewy with moisture. His muscled chest twitching with power. Her mouth ran dry like a desert while she went wet with need.

"Shiloh, are you all right?"

She bit her bottom lip to keep it from trembling.

"I-I've come home. To apologize."

"Home? You're not home yet."

"Wh-what do you mean?"

He opened his arms and waved her to enter his space. Joy bubbled over, and she ran to him, where he picked her up to hold her in his protective embrace. "Now, you're home."

She closed her eyes. Tears overflowed their moorings, burning hot trails down her cheeks. "I'm so sorry. I've been an idiot. I'm such a hot mess, I don't know why you still want to have anything to do with me."

"I love you. It doesn't get any simpler."

Sniffing then laughing, she eased back to gaze up at her mate's beautiful face. There, behind his crystal-green eyes, she found the proof of his words.

Leaning in, he kissed her, gently at first then his longing and relief barreled through her like a freight train. When he released her, he took a step into the foyer, his chest heaving. She followed him, entranced. He walked farther inside, to the couch in his living room. She sat beside him.

"I don't wanna spook you or anything, but you're inside my apartment. You're sitting on my couch."

"I know." Sliding her arm around his waist, she

snuggled against his warm, smooth body. "I've made some real progress today with my healing."

He hoisted her onto his lap, and every nuance of his need touched her through the towel while he nibbled on her exposed shoulder. "I'll have to thank Zamirah in the morning."

"Oh, well, I kinda shooed her away, actually."

He stopped his feasting and gave her a puzzled look. "What?"

"Yeah, I'll have to apologize to her, too. Safe to say, I behaved badly."

"Hmm, I wouldn't worry. She's a forgiving woman. So what's caused this turnaround?"

"I was visited by my spirit guide. Had no idea I had one until tonight," she half mumbled to herself. "Although, she did say I always had you, so she wasn't needed during the time I was held captive. She wasn't needed...until I left you." Ashamed, she lowered her eyes. "She's a wise one. She showed me how skewed my perspective has been because of...him."

"Then I must thank *her*!" He turned his attention to creating little fires of love along her collarbone, but she would not be distracted from what she needed to say.

"Parker, listen." Cupping his face in her hands,

she stared him square in the eyes. "I'm sorry for so much. For not seeking to understand our rituals. For running from you, again. We've known each other for two years. I should have trusted in our bond. Whatever you would say or do would be for my benefit. I should've known you'd never hurt me."

He laid his hands over hers, squeezing lightly. "I'm sorry I didn't listen better to you. I never meant to hurt you. I only wanted to show the world I loved you and you were under my protection. I wanted you to know in no uncertain terms you'll never have to worry about your safety again. I've been told by women my dominant personality doesn't leave room for other's opinions or ways. It's my way or no way. Probably why I've been single all this time. From here on out, it's *our* way."

"I like the sound of that," she said, her voice thick with desire. He lowered his lips to hers to exploit her response. When he finally released her, nerve endings rapid fired, and she squirmed, pressing herself on his hardened cock. Her need of him eclipsed all reason. If she didn't get a piece of him within the next few minutes, she thought she'd go insane. "Parker?"

"Hmmm?"

She slithered her way down to the floor to sit

before his legs. Her hands trailed up his shins, over his knees, and under the towel to peel it open, revealing the object of her desire. "I'm so done with talking right now."

Leaning forward, she guided her mouth to meet her hands as they wrapped around his shaft in a sensual embrace. She groaned, tasting her mate and wanting so much more. As she licked, sucked, and took him deeply into her mouth, he growled, cupping her head in his hands to slow her frantic pace. She luxuriated in the silky warmth of his throbbing penis, knowing he would soon use it to bring her to the most exquisite climax.

"Baby, you're killing me. Come here." He stood and brought her with him. "You have way too many clothes on. Let me help you with that."

Piece by piece, he removed her clothes to reveal a body in stark, disfigured-alabaster contrast to his own. But she didn't care anymore how damaged she was. He made her feel like the most precious gem in the jewelry case. With her T-shirt and bra torn clear off by his teeth, he traced delicate circles around her breasts until he reached her dark-pink nipples. He used his tongue to flick the hardened buds, to which she responded by mewling. and tossed her head back. He charted a trail down to her waist, where he wasted no time unzipping and pulling down her pants and panties, soaked with arousal.

"Your skin, mmm." His voice vibrated against her belly. "The perfect complement to mine. "Do you know you have constellations of freckles all over your body? Here's one." Just above her hip bone sat a small freckle, which he kissed. Then he moved to another by her belly button, and two others on her rib cage. "I'm not sure of the name of this one, but I'm sure it has one. I'll have to search for it on the Internet someday." He stood tall before her, his smoldering eyes setting her soul on fire. "Shiloh, I'm taking you to my bed now, and we're not leaving it until we're too sore to move, so then we'll have to stay in my bed some more."

"I'm up for the challenge." Her face flushed with desire.

He swept her up in his arms. In just a few strides, laid her upon his bed. Like a canopy, he hovered above her, and she took him all in. This gargantuan man, so strong, so confident, so virile, had eyes only for her. She was ready to give everything she had to him. Raising her arms, she beckoned him to lie upon her. He obeyed. As skin touched skin, a sigh escaped her lips. *So blessed*. She wrapped her legs around him, opening herself for the ultimate union.

He rubbed against her but wouldn't enter. Instead, he rested his hardened shaft against her while focusing on her face. Tangling his fingers in her hair, he spoke in a voice hoarse with emotion. "When your wolf called to mine that first time, I came, expecting to rescue you from your hell. I was shocked to wake up the next morning to realize what felt so real was only a dream. Each night, I'd go, hoping to find a way to save you, and I'd fall deeper in love with you. Now, with you here, *free*, as a woman, I've fallen in love all over again. What man, what wolf, gets so lucky as to fall in love twice with the same one?"

"I do. We're doubly blessed."

He kissed her lips softly then teased her with his gentle prodding. "This time, you're in charge. What do you want, baby?"

Restless with need, she wrestled him underneath her and clasped his hands to bring them above his head. "I'm gonna ride you, cowboy. Show you how very blessed I feel." Leaning in for a fiery kiss, she rubbed her hardened nipples against his chest. She moaned, writhing on top of him, creating waves of shivery sensations up and down her body.

"Please, let me touch you, sweetness."

She sat up, pulling his hands with her, and laid them upon her breasts. Giving him a wicked smirk, she eased herself on his stiffened cock. Inch by excruciating inch, she lowered and raised herself again. He growled low as though warning her he didn't have much control left. Just the way she wanted him because she had little time left before she climaxed. Slick from her heightened arousal, she quickened the pace, arching her back as he kneaded her breasts and twisted her nipples, sending her crying out, skyrocketing into oblivion. He moved his hands to grab her hips and bucked beneath her as he howled his own release.

She collapsed on top of him, sweaty and spent. "Don't move. Don't do anything. Just stay inside me a little while longer."

"No argument from me." He continued to pulse inside her for a few more minutes, creating shock waves deep inside her belly.

Dozing off, she awakened several times during the night to find Parker bringing her body to flaming-hot levels. Other times, she scorched him.

"I don't know about you, Parker, but I think I've reached your goal. I'm sore in all the right places. I guess we get to stay in bed all day."

He traced lazy circles low on her spine then kissed the top of her head. "You know we have to open up at seven, right?"

With a stealthy hand, she grasped one of the pillows tossed haphazardly about during their lovemaking and swatted him on the head.

Chapter Nine

Bread & Butter was a madhouse! A zoo! By noon, Parker had already called Bryan to place another full-stock order. He figured he might have to do this a couple of more times before everyone felt secure with their stocked pantries and refrigerators. At this rate, he'd have enough money banked to be able to build an addition onto the store next year.

Shiloh was a real trouper, too. Neither had slept for more than a couple of hours the night before, and his store opened way too early in the morning. But who needed sleep when the love of your life, your mate was nearby? Cupid had shot a bull's-eye on his heart.

Half of his day, despite talking to customers or re-stocking the shelves, had been consumed with images of Shiloh naked in his bed, her fiery-red hair splayed across the pillow, her body open for him and him alone. The rest of the time, he'd snatched glimpses of her as she wove her way through the throngs or took control of the register. Every so often, her eyes would meet his, and she'd beamed with a full-on blush, exposing the sexiest dimples at the corners of her pouty mouth. He visited the freezer multiple times during the day just to get his hard-on under control.

By evening, as the last of the customers dwindled to a few, he noticed the toll the day had taken on her, and he wasn't happy. He set aside the loaves of bread he held and walked to her.

"Hey, you did awesome today." He hugged her then massaged her shoulders. "But you seem a bit out of sorts. What can I do for you?"

"All these people today, being inside for so long.... I need to get out. Run. If I don't, my wolf will tear this place apart."

"I totally understand." He untied her apron and then his own. "I'm ready if you are."

"Parker, I don't want to hurt your feelings, but I meant I need to run alone. Just me in the wilderness."

"I can't let—" He held up his hand. "No, let me rephrase. I'd be very uncomfortable if you didn't let me at least follow you from a distance. Can you let me?"

"I'm impressed by your desire to retrain your brain." She kissed him lightly on the lips. "Yes, I can meet you halfway. Thank you for loving me."

"You never have to thank me, sweetheart. You deserve my love and so much more." He whispered a kiss upon her lips and lightly tapped her ass. "You have the head start. Go for it!"

Her golden eyes glistened as she shifted into her wolf. Chuffing and growling, she frolicked about then dashed out the open front door. He laughed, shaking his head while turning out the lights and locking up. He used the inside stairs to access his apartment then jumped off his balcony to race after her.

She'd never know how much control he'd used to keep from going ballistic at her desire to run alone. She didn't need or want an alpha mate in her life. She'd made it abundantly clear. A dominant, though, could be just as strong-willed. It would take time, but he vowed to evolve into her kind of mate. It could be a good thing. Nothing wrong with autonomy in a relationship.

Loping along her scented trail, he picked up another's. Elk. There was a second, no a third, all in the area. He wondered if his mate fancied a late-night meal, and quickened his gait to catch up to her to ask. Though the prey's scents grew stronger, he couldn't see them anywhere.

Shiloh's slender frame appeared frozen, like a statue, in a distant clearing. His heart skipped a beat. What a magnificent creature she was! He admired her piercing gaze and predatory stance. But what had she found? *Damn it!* He couldn't see! She shifted her stance to face the opposite direction, and her low growl reached his ears. Concern and confusion took hold as he stalked closer, hoping to discover the object of her attention.

Where are the elk? If they were where their scent was guiding him, they had to be wearing magical invisibility cloaks, because they were nowhere to be seen. He continued scanning the area, but his gaze returned to her for some clear indication as to what was happening. Shiloh retreated, spinning multiple times. Then, it all became clear.

Those invisible elk weren't elk at all.

One by one, gray wolves came out from under elk's clothing, as it were, and rushed from the thick underbrush to surround Shiloh. Growling, yipping, baring teeth. They taunted their prey. Outrage coursed through Parker's veins, blinding him for a moment before he raced over and leapt into action to save his mate. He pounced onto the back of the nearest wolf, clamping down hard on his neck. He twisted and shook the smaller animal then tossed it against the side of a tree. It lay on the ground, unconscious, bleeding heavily from its wounds.

Parker had just enough time to catch Shiloh's attention, to let her know he was there. She'd be all right. The other wolves sprinted to double-team him. These wolves were smaller, yes, and one had been easy to put down, but two at a time would present a bit of a problem. They both leapt in the air, pounding him to the ground. Each took a side, biting, tearing.

Howling, Shiloh pounced on top of the pile, managing to pull one off him. That gave him the leverage he needed to wrestle the other away, subsequently inflicting deadly damage to the wolf's throat. When he turned to check on Shiloh, he found her scuffling on the ground with the last wolf. He wanted to kill the bastard, but when he caught her eye, she shook her muzzle, continuing to spar. So, taking a deep breath, he hung back, keeping a watchful eye on her progress.

This wasn't just a rogue group in disguise on the prowl. She knew these wolves, and by the way she tore into this one, she had a score to settle. She appeared to be in it to the end. His end.

With one final bite at the wolf's neck, she sank her teeth into his throat, then walked with the limp body to Parker, dropping him at his feet, howling a long, mournful song. Then she dropped to the ground and curled up in a ball, snuffling.

Parker shifted from his wolf to stroke her head. Wrapping her up in his arms, he lifted her onto his lap. "Shiloh, sweetheart, put your wolf away, baby."

She complied but remained tightly coiled, her body racked with sobs. He wouldn't try to stop her. She'd earned every one of those tears. But he'd do his best to comfort her then let her know she was alive. "It's all right now. It's okay. It's over. You've won."

She sniffed, hiccupped then lifted her face to meet his. "Do you know how many days I wished I could kill Josiah? Silas? All of those beastly men for what they did to me?"

He nodded and gentled away the steady stream of tears from her cheeks, but didn't say a word. There was so much more to come.

"I would sit all day long, with nothing to do but plan my escape and revenge." She sniffed. "I would devise all sorts of wicked ways to drag out their deaths and how I'd deliver the final blow." She lowered her head, leaning against his chest. "After killing them daydream upon daydream, I'd emerge victorious, pumped up, hopeful. You know?"

"Uh-huh." He swept aside strands of red hair to tuck behind her ear.

"But, now, I did it. I mean I really killed Silas. And...and I don't feel anything close to what I thought I would. While I was doing it, my teeth piercing his flesh, I felt invincible. Like I'd just saved the world from a deviant. But once he stopped moving...." She pounded her fists against his chest, wailing anew. "I'm no better than a murderer. Vile. Just like him. Just like Josiah."

He strengthened his hold on her, hoping to banish the cruel words she'd used to describe herself. "Shiloh, don't ever let me hear you compare yourself to those demented lowlifes again. They came here looking for you. They shielded themselves from tracker detection just so they could get to you. What do you think they wanted?"

She shrugged.

"Oh, you know damn well what they wanted. Only, this time, you wouldn't let them turn you into their victim. You're a fighter. A warrior!"

"A warrior, huh?" She wiped her cheeks with her shredded shirt.

"You defended yourself and came away victorious. Now you can say you're truly free."

"I *am* free." Satisfaction washed over her face as she took a deep cleansing breath.

"I'm so proud of you."

"Thanks. I can always count on you, can't I?" She peered up at him, and he nodded. "So can I count on you to give me the shirt off your back? I gotta blow my nose."

He howled with laughter as he tore his shirt off for her to use. "Do you think we can salvage the rest of this evening?"

"I have enough adrenaline coursing through me for the both of us. I say we finish the run and have ferocious sex on top of the bluff I found the other day."

"I can definitely go along with that plan."

She stood up and handed him the spent T-shirt.

"Oh, thanks, but it's biodegradable. It can stay right here."

He shifted. She followed suit. Together, they ran to the edge of the pack lands to Shiloh's overhang. Once there, they returned to their human forms to make love like animals. This time, though, something seemed different. Her desire for Parker, to touch him, or even just to be near him, had intensified after the skirmish to such a level, she thought she'd crawl out of her skin.

Sweaty and breathless, they tussled on the grassy

patch above the cave. Once on top, Shiloh eyed Parker's fleshy part above the collarbone. It tempted her, so she bent over him and suckled on it while he thrust into her at a frantic pace. She had an insatiable desire to clamp down as her first orgasm rolled through her like a roller coaster. Was Parker feeling the same way?

She sat up as he continued to plunge deep inside her. Not sure of where it came from, she cried out, "Bite me, baby."

His eyes widened. His body froze. "What? Are you sure you know what you're asking me to do? I don't have to."

"But I do. You have to, too. I'm ready. So ready."

He sat up, still inside her, holding her body against his. She rocked on him, creating new waves of orgasmic shivers across her body. Groaning, he nuzzled her neck while she did the same. As her climax hit her hard, she bit down on his upper shoulder. His body stiffened as he came with her. Pain shot through her shoulder for the briefest of moments, followed by a surge of peace.

"Mine," she gushed as he growled the same.

He leaned his forehead against hers, breathing hard, laughing. "I believe we just made our relationship official."

"I believe so." She closed her eyes. "We're mated. I'm all yours. And...and I'm okay with that now."

He leaned back, cupped her face in his hands to stare into her eyes with mock seriousness. "I'm all yours now, too. So if any women come sniffing around, will you save me?"

"Oh, most definitely! Those ladies better steer clear!" She poked at his ribs, giggling for the first time in what seemed like forever. It felt great to have such a lighthearted moment together. She knew it'd be the first of many.

"Come on," he said, standing them both up. He gathered their clothes. "Let's go on home." He held out hers to take, but she refused them.

"Wait."

"What? What is it?"

Wrapping her arms around his waist, she held him close. "Now, I'm home."

Sign up for the Decadent Publishing Newsletter here
http://eepurl.com/SQ75f **and never miss stories like:**

Disquieted Souls by Deena Remiel

Chapter One

Greyson slid his spent shot glass toward the edge of the bar counter. "One more, Gee, and make it a double."

His demand only bought him a disapproving glare from the self-righteous bastard. Well, maybe that was a little harsh. After all, he was one of a token few who didn't treat him like a pariah. Him and Drew, anyway. But such a look. He wasn't his father, although Gee'd practically raised his sorry ass from birth. So what if he wanted to get shit-faced after a long week of tracking? Surveillance could take a lot out of a man or Wolf.

"Gonna honor my request, my overly protective friend? My money's still good here, ain't it?"

"You'll have a hamburger and fried pickles with your alcohol."

"Yes, sir." He snickered and popped a toothpick in his mouth to gnaw on.

He knew better than to argue with the old Bear and flashed him a toothy grin. His motto when it came to Gee? If he grinned at a bear long enough, the bear

136

would eventually return the smile. He'd been grinning at the man for close to thirty years now, and he'd yet to see his goal realized. As the man of few words left to put in the order, Greyson hung his head. He almost never saw Gee at the bar, and he had to pick today to make an appearance. A week spent on edge, tracking an elusive rogue with no results to show for it, ruffled his fur something fierce. Lots of booze or a good screw would settle his disgruntled Wolf down. Seeing as no woman in the town would get within ten feet of him, he figured downing a couple of doubles, at least, were in his future.

He checked his reflection and then around the room through the mirrored backsplash behind the beer taps. There wasn't a person in the place who didn't look upon him as some kind of weird anomaly. For as long as he'd lived in Los Lobos, his unique appearance set him apart, and some made it quite clear his odd features made it uncomfortable to be around. Drew, Betty, Gee, and even Ryker were the only ones who'd seen past the pale skin and stark-white hair. Past the peculiar eyes—one indigo blue and the other amber with gold flecks. They saw right to the soul within.

As he'd grown, Greyson loved listening to Gee tell

137

the story of how he came to be part of the Tao pack. He'd been left to die in the wilderness by a mother apparently not interested in caring for the runt of her litter. The Alpha's son, Drew, found him then Gee unofficially adopted him. As the two young boys grew up together, Drew would vehemently defend him against the other young ones in the pack, but it only seemed to exacerbate the teasing and relentless bullying by some when his friend wasn't around. Greyson realized soon enough he would have to stand on his own. His violent reaction to a bout of harassment scared the persistent young guns and served to finally put them in their place.

When he was old enough, he'd moved to the fringe of the pack lands, where he felt he wouldn't be subjected to any more possible taunts and jeers from bigoted Wolves on their way up the pack ladder. Of course, being a newly minted adult, he'd gotten resistance to break out on his own from Gee, but after Magnum expelled Drew, there was no reason to stay close to town. So he built a cabin on the very plot of land where he'd been dumped as a pup, hoping by living there he could someday learn of his mother's true motivations. A part of him hoped his birth pack lived somewhere nearby, and they'd show up one day for a reunion of sorts to put all his questions to rest.

Gee returned with a basket of fried pickles and a hamburger. He frowned and growled. "Eat."

"All right, all right. What about that drink?"

The were-bear grabbed the bottle of tequila and poured.

"Double, please. In fact, you know what? Just pour four shots-worth into a glass for me. Okay?"

He raised a brow, shook his head, but poured anyway.

"Thank you so much. Don't worry. I'll leave the way I came—running on all fours."

With a smirk and a snort, Gee turned on his heel and disappeared into the inner sanctum of his office. Of course, that left an opening for a group of idiots sitting at the table directly to Greyson's left to behave all sorts of stupid, making derogatory comments under their breath, but loud enough for him to hear. He'd never seen them in the bar before, but not recognizing them didn't mean anything. So many Wolves had returned home. If they were in Los Lobos, Drew, Ryker and the others knew they were there. Self-consciously, he put his sunglasses on. Maybe giving them one less thing to comment on would make them move on to someone else.

With half a burger downed and a full glass of tequila tossed back, he was ready for their imminent attack. No sooner had he wiped his mouth with a napkin did they get up from their seats and approached. He breathed in slowly, deeply, deliberately to calm his ruffled Wolf.

"Hey, freak." The apparent leader of the pack of goons nudged his shoulder with a few fingers. He noted the latent strength in them but refused to respond in the hope they'd get bored and leave. "It's dark. Why you covering up them pretty eyes of yours?"

Though every fiber of his being thrummed and ached for him to let lose all the pent-up adrenaline on the asshole, Greyson didn't turn around, flinch, or remove his sunglasses, either. "Oh, I don't let just anyone gaze upon these beauties. I was waiting for you to come over here. These babies are for your eyes only, kitten."

That sparked a flurry of growls and snarls from the group, and the high-strung leader tossed a few chairs out of his way. The few other customers in the bar issued a collective warning growl. It was nice to know they were in his corner, should the need arise.

Greyson took his time and stood, showing the buffoons exactly what they were getting into. He stood a good head and shoulders taller than them and was nearly twice as wide. "Now before you go pouncing on me in that crazed, hormonal way of yours, let me tell you a little secret. You're in Gee's place. He doesn't take kindly to barroom brawls. Costs too much to fix and makes him a bit angry. So, if you wanna piss off the big old bear, go for it. In all honesty, if I were you, I'd leave *me* the fuck alone." He turned and then resumed his seat to finish his burger.

His assailants huffed and puffed as they surrounded him, and the first guy stuffed his pointed nose right up to Greyson's cheek. Through gritted teeth he hissed, "You're lucky, freak. This time. Next time, though, your ass is mine."

"My ass likes women. Sorry. But I think a few of your groupies might be into that kinda thing."

Another round of howling and Gee appeared with a bat in the doorway to the kitchen. The pack of idiots took the hint and left. He finished his burger, popped the last of the fried pickles in his mouth at a leisurely pace, and wiped his mouth again. Gee returned to the kitchen without a word. He'd give those jerk-offs a bit to clear out of town before he left for home. It wasn't a question of fear. He could easily obliterate each one of them without so much as blinking an eye. As a group, though, they were probably lethal.

The tequila finally kicked in and blunted his ability to absorb visual and auditory information. *Perfect. Now to head home and crash.* He tucked a few dollars under his glass and eased off the barstool, not sure if his feet would remember to move. He'd do much better to shift now. Four legs were better than two when he was drunk.

A simple shrug, like an involuntary shiver, then his clothes and body morphed into the Wolf who'd been denied the thrill of the kill all week long. With a gruff snuffle, he pushed the door open with his snout, looked all around with bleary eyes to check if the coast was clear before trotting down the dirt road, into the forest, toward his home.

As he loped along the winding path to the front porch, numbness crept across his haunches. It was only a matter of time before his legs followed suit. He shifted to his human form, took out his key, and unlocked the door after a number of failed attempts. As he poured himself into his bed, his last thoughts before passing out were, "Mission *not* accomplished. May you find the rogue fucker and kill him good and dead tomorrow."

***

It didn't take Willow five minutes to figure out the day's photo shoot was going to be a nonstop pain in the ass. Not only did the imbeciles at *Fashion Forward Magazine* contract two of the most annoying models, but the two most annoying models who couldn't stand each other. What were they thinking?

They weren't. They didn't give a rat's ass who slept with whom and then got dumped, or who had a restraining order against another. It came down to the almighty dollar. These models took phenomenal photos, so the fact they despised each other at the moment was irrelevant.

This week, Willow was stuck with the drama king and queen who never grew past their high school years. Carter and Cassandra were known to have been tight about a year before. After a few times catching him in bed with other models, she'd had enough and made no bones about spreading news of his philandering. Both held grudges forever. From the looks on their faces as they exited makeup and hair, today promised to be a grudge match for the ages.

Taking a deep breath and pretending not to notice, Willow headed toward the Fort Union Trading

Post, a historic landmark in North Dakota and site for the day's fashion shoot. While waiting for the final touch-ups, a meadowlark flew past and landed on a light pole. She swung her camera up to her eye and focused in. Engrossed in her subject, only a harsh tap on her shoulder jolted her to reality. Her passion for nature photography would have to be sidelined until her day job released her.

"They don't pay you for lovely pictures of birds, Will. They pay you for lovely pictures of these two immature imbeciles of the human species. Come on."

"Can't say you don't speak the truth, Harry." Her lighting man laughed along with her as they made their way to the staging area.

Throughout the next three hours, she snapped hundreds of pictures, if not thousands, of Carter and Cassandra looking hot, sexy, and posing in erotically charged positions for the swimsuit issue. In between shots, their hatred toward each other was palpable, but once the cameras were rolling, their sexually charged chemistry ignited the scene. That's how it'd been all week. Didn't matter where they set the backdrop. Nuclear war was imminent unless a camera was shooting.

"Two to one, those two will be fucking like

bunnies at the end of this."

"Jesus, Harry! Could you be any *more* crass?" She took a long swig from her can of cola. "I wouldn't take that bet in a million years, though, 'cause I agree with you. Okay, folks! Break's over! Let's get this show on the road! I wanna see hot! I wanna see sexy! I wanna feel as though there's no way I could ever walk down a beach or swim in a pool or even walk into a...a trading post without wearing one of those swimsuits! Go!"

When the last shot had been taken, everyone clapped and hugged. She even got hugs and a comment from Cassandra. "You are one of the best photographers we've ever worked with. It's been a great week overall, for sure, but we're exhausted. So glad it's finally over."

The greatest you've ever worked with? That's because every time you objected to something, which was every freakin' shot, I had to comply with your wishes, as per my supervisor's directive, you immature brat. Or, I could've ignored you and lost my job.

"Any time! Good luck with your next job. See you around." She flashed a courteous grin, calculating how fast she could get out of there. As she packed up her gear, she heard a racket from the makeshift dressing room. She laughed and shook her head. It never ended! With her bags and lighting safely stowed, she hopped in her SUV and shoved off. In her rearview mirror she watched as Carter and Cassandra ambled out of the dressing room a bit mussed and arm in arm. The tabloids were gonna have a field day with the latest development.

Back in her motel room, with a poor excuse for takeout pizza resting on the bed and a cold beer on the bedside table, Willow rested her weary bones and closed her eyes. It wasn't that she was tired from the day's work. She was exhausted from all the bullshit she'd had to put up with since landing this gig. When she'd first started in the fashion photography business, she didn't notice all the nuances of relationships and political power plays. That was four years ago. Now, at twenty-eight, she was burned out and ready to give it all up. Admittedly, her life was deep in the crapper, and she struggled with how to crawl out. If she had to bartend to make ends meet, she would.

She sat up tall, her hooded eyes snapped wide open, her brain, instantly alert with equal parts excitement and horror. "I do believe...I've decided...I might be done with this bullshit career." The thrill of a possible change set her heart racing and mind on full-tilt. *What exactly am I saying here?* "Whoa, whoa, whoa, my dear, let's not make any rash decisions. Sleep on it. Take a break. You're due for a vacation anyway. See how you feel when you return. Right? Right." The fashion industry, with all its plastic models and phony, two-faced people would still be there when she returned. *If* she returned.

She chomped down on a doughy slice and took a long draw of beer. Yeah, that decision sat well with her. There was nothing pressing at home in California. No animals to look after. Her parents were traipsing through Africa for the year, and her brother and sister were workaholics. No jobs coming up for her until next month. It was the perfect opportunity to go off the grid, relax, reevaluate her life, and nurture her passion by taking as many pictures as she wanted of nature.

She leaped off the bed and grabbed her laptop to search for places to camp. She'd had enough of North Dakota, so she went south with her search. South Dakota had the Black Hills National Forest. They had campgrounds where she could pitch a tent or set up an RV. Within the hour, she had reservations for four weeks starting the next day. Now all she needed was the equipment and gear to set up her home away from home. She'd pick them all up, along with the pull-along pop-up camper, once across the state line at an RV rental center.

Camping and hiking were second nature to her. She'd done all sorts with her family for years from tent to camper, even survivalist style. She picked off a piece of pepperoni from the last slice. As she popped it into her mouth, she recalled a fond childhood memory, when they attempted to make pizza over a campfire. Her parents had their moments of coolness. Not many, but a few. Once they and her siblings scattered across the fifty states and explored more urban pursuits, she still had the rugged bug deep inside her and managed to continue camping on her own, but never for this long. *This is gonna be one hell of an adventure!*

The next morning, she awoke with the sun and got an early start on her trek to the other Dakota. A stop at the local Laundromat gave her time to eat some breakfast with Harry first.

"You're really doing this?"

"Yes, I really am." She folded a piece of bacon into her mouth, talking as she chewed. "It's no big deal. I'm a longtime hardcore camper, my friend."

"But for a month? You're a strange bird."

"Honestly, I've never camped for this long, but I'm sure it'll be fine. I'll be taking as many pictures of those dang birds as I want, by the way. And elk and rabbits and trees and insects and...."

"I get it. I get it! You want to be one with nature."

"No, I just want to take pictures of it. I don't mind living beside nature, though. It's a far cry from those neurotic, infantile people we have to deal with day in and day out. Harry, I gotta do this or I'll lose my soul. It's practically gone as it is. I barely recognize who I am anymore."

He reached out a hand to cover hers and squeezed. "So, do you need me to do anything while you're Grizzly Willow?"

She rolled her eyes. "Actually, yes. Just one thing. Can you mail this rent check out for me on the date I wrote on the envelope? I don't think I'll be anywhere near a post office."

"Sure, no problem."

She tapped her napkin against her lips and placed it on the remains of her pancakes. "Well, I gotta run. Laundry's probably done, and they're the only clothes I have."

They stood at the same time and hugged hard. She didn't have close friends. Who did in the fashion industry? But Harry was as close as she'd get. "Listen, if you need anything, call me. Don't let your phone's

149

battery run out. You hear me?" She nodded. "And if it gets too much, haul your ass home."

"Got it. Thanks so much for everything, Harry. You're the only *real* person I know in this crazy, effed-up business. Promise you'll remember to keep it real. All right?"

"Promise." One last hug and she left him to finish his coffee.

Clothes were scorched dry and ready for folding. She placed them right into her suitcase, zipped it up, and called the RV place where she reserved the latest model of a small pop-up camper equipped with a sink and a double-burner stove. She'd be living in style in the Black Hills of South Dakota!